Elim Henry D'Avigdor

Glamour

Vol. II

Elim Henry D'Avigdor

Glamour
Vol. II

ISBN/EAN: 9783337067014

Printed in Europe, USA, Canada, Australia, Japan

Cover: Foto ©Andreas Hilbeck / pixelio.de

More available books at **www.hansebooks.com**

GLAMOUR.

A Novel.

BY

WANDERER,

AUTHOR OF 'FAIR DIANA,' 'ACROSS COUNTRY,' ETC.

IN THREE VOLUMES.

VOL. II.

ARDVA·QV&·PVLCRA

LONDON:

SWAN SONNENSCHEIN AND CO.,

PATERNOSTER SQUARE.

1885.

CONTENTS OF VOL. II.

GLAMOUR.

CHAPTER XVII.

THE PLUNGE.

By dint of hard work, work which amused Ronald without exciting him, the play was written out on the Tuesday night, and the next day all the actors came to copy their parts. The first rehearsal was fixed for Thursday. Edith was gradually regaining confidence, and found to her surprise that Ronald continued to address her with the greatest cordiality, which even she could hardly take to be assumed. She attributed his kindness to his gentle and forgiving nature. She was consoled by the thought that he was inclined to forget her flippancy and wickedness if he could, and her appearance improved as her unhappiness diminished. For Edith's face showed trouble at once; her eyes were transparent as the clearest water, and she could seldom entirely conceal her feelings, though she might do her best to repress them.

On the Thursday afternoon, a sofa was moved into the boudoir, and Ronald was carried downstairs in an arm-chair. There was a good deal of fun and nonsense over this first rehearsal, for not one of the actors knew his or her part, except Teresina, who played the worldly mother to perfection. Mrs. Lascelles was in and out of the room during the rehearsal, and Ronald watched it with much amusement from the sofa, frequently interrupting the actors by his stage directions, and prompting them continually. When at last they had got through the piece, tea was brought in, and Ronald was quite overwhelmed with attentions. But Edith found herself alone with him when Teresina had dragged away the rest to the old disused nursery, where all sorts of old rags, dresses, bits of carpet, and other sundries were stored, out of which she wished to make up the costumes for the play. Edith stayed behind on purpose. She felt that she would not know peace till she had begged Ronald's forgiveness. She approached the couch timidly.

'Mr. Lascelles,' she began, 'I have been wanting to speak to you so much.'

'Why *Mr.* Lascelles?' asked Ronald, smiling. 'You used to call me Ronald.'

'I cannot now,' she said, blushing. 'Oh! if you only knew how sorry I am.'

'Sorry for *me?* There is no occasion, Edith dear. I am getting on famously; I shall be about in a fortnight.'

'I don't mean only about your poor leg,' continued

18—2

Edith, clasping her hands. 'Oh, can you ever forgive me?'

'What for? What on earth do you mean?' asked Ronald. 'Sit down and tell me all about it, Edith.' He stretched out his hand to her, and pointed to a chair by the sofa. 'As well now as any other time,' thought he.

Edith sat down, and looked at his thin face, still drawn with pain. Her large blue eyes were full of tenderness and pity; there was a teardrop just trembling on the long lashes, her lips were parted, and the declining sun lighted up her fair hair with a golden ray. She might have been the model for Correggio's repentant Magdalen.

'I was so foolish—so wicked!' she said at last, flushing. 'I flirted dreadfully with that horrid Marchese, and answered pertly when you told me of it.'

'But you threw him over afterwards, Edith, and we made it up at supper! Do you not remember?'

He took her unresisting hand, and held it in a gentle clasp.

'Of course I remember!' replied Edith. 'I can never forget that evening. You were very good, and very kind; and I was horrid to let that man go on till he actually thought he had a *right* to dance with me! Oh, I know all about the duel, Ronald!'

'Do you?' asked he, still holding her hand; 'who told you?'

'I found it out—all out—gradually. I got a bit from one, and a bit from some one else, and put them all together——'

'Like a Chinese puzzle?' suggested Ronald.

'How can you laugh about it? It was too dreadful. The Marchese insulted you on purpose, and then you pretended to have a quarrel at the Club——'

'We *did* have a quarrel at the Club,' interrupted Ronald again.

'It was all pretence, I know that. And then you went out and let the horrible man shoot at you, all because I had been foolish and naughty. He might have killed you.'

At the thought of what might have happened, Edith withdrew her hand and raised her pocket-handkerchief to her eyes. She was no coquette. If she had been a little more experienced, she would have known that tears did not suit her at all. Very few faces are improved by them, and hers was certainly not of the number.

'Don't cry over it now,' said Ronald. 'You see he did not kill me.'

'But he hurt you dreadfully, and you were so generous that you would not shoot back! If I had been in your place, I am sure I should have shot him dead.'

'How could I kill a man for admiring you, Edith dear? It is such a very pardonable offence. Of course I was obliged to let him off. I should have to make shambles of Portino if I once began killing your admirers !'

'Now you are talking nonsense and laughing at me again,' said Edith. 'You do not seem to care one bit.'

Nor did he. That was the worst of it. For the life of him, Ronald could not look at the situation seriously. He was rather amused, and much interested in watching Edith, and in giving her what the French call *la réplique;* but he spoke and felt as if he were outside it all, and had not any real practical concern in the matter.

'Why should I care,' said he flippantly, 'now I am getting all right again, and the nicest girl in Portino comes on purpose to amuse me? Lots of fellows would envy my luck.'

Edith grew almost angry.

'You keep making silly compliments when I am

trying to tell you how deeply sorry and grieved I am for the mischief I have done. It is unkind. I shall begin to fear that you will not forgive me, and that you bear malice secretly, though you conceal it with a lot of rubbishy fine speeches.'

'Indeed,' said Ronald sincerely, 'you are wrong. I do not think I have anything to forgive. This duel has made me quite a notoriety in the place. Surely such renown is worth so trifling a wound?'

'That is not all!' exclaimed Edith. 'Your mother told me that they would not give you the leave you asked for to get well. That is my fault, too! Oh, I only wish I had never gone to that ball! Fancy having spoilt your whole life by my thoughtlessness! How can I ever make up for it?'

'Very easily, dear Edith,' said Ronald, calmly taking advantage of the opening offered him, and again clasping her hand. 'Very easily indeed; that is, if you like.'

'How?' asked Edith eagerly. 'Of course I shall like.'

'I am not quite sure of that,' answered Ronald. 'You might not like, after all. In fact, I don't see why you should.' He hesitated still before he took the final plunge. There was still time to retreat with all honours. He dropped again into his bantering tone. 'And if you don't make up for it that way, I am sure I shall never forgive you, never—never!'

'You are laughing at me again, Mr. Lascelles,' said Edith, trying to withdraw her hand. But Ronald held it fast.

'There is another crime! Why, you will have to pay a cumulative penalty! My *father* is Mr. Lascelles; *my* name is Ronald, and always has been since I carried you pick-a-back to Banbury Cross.'

'You never thought that the little girl you played with would send you to your death and destroy your prospects.'

'She has done neither. Prospects?' said Ronald, bitterly and seriously enough. 'Prospects? pah! I never had any at Somerset House; never could have any, if I had stopped there twenty years. And as to sending me to my death, why here I am, alive and kicking—no, not exactly kicking. I can't kick at present; but I shall, soon.'

'Poor man! and all my fault!' exclaimed Edith. 'I believe you talk lightly of your prospects now, because I have destroyed them. I believe you are only laughing and talking nonsense to prevent my thinking about my wickedness. You make light of it to relieve my mind. But you cannot do that, however you may disguise your feelings.'

The conversation was drifting away from sentiment, and Ronald felt that if he did not make an effort, the chance would be lost. He could not hold her hand much longer.

She looked very nice again, now that her tears

had dried. There was a delicate soft colour on her cheeks, and as she had her back to the window, the nose was not particularly prominent. A few stray curls were still lighted up by a golden sun. Her graceful figure, stooping a little forward, was clad in a very well-fitting dress of soft brown cashmere. Her snow-white collar was scarcely whiter than the little bit of neck visible above it. There was a fascinating turn in that slender neck as she looked away towards the door for a moment, and a magnetic power about those soft, downy curls by the small shell-like ear.

Positively, she was more than merely pretty, thought Ronald. There was a tenderness and sweetness about her he had never suspected. His mother's plans were forgotten. If he had remembered them, perhaps he would not have yielded to the impulse of the moment. But surely the two would not have been left so long alone together unless there had been some little scheming upstairs, beyond the scheming necessary to make a few old rags do for stage costumes.

Perhaps the design was a little deeper and more complicated than Ronald supposed. For the time, at any rate, he thought of no design, and his mind was no longer troubled with doubts. The pretty head against the light, the golden waves of hair, the graceful figure, the slender hand clasped in his own, the blue eyes gazing wistfully into space—seeking to soothe the pain they had inflicted, to make good the fancied damage they had done—these only were before him. All else was nothing. Raising his head from the pillow, he drew her towards him and placed his lips close to her little ear.

'You can make it all up to me, Edith dear,' he whispered, and imprinted a soft kiss on the white neck.

'Ronald!' exclaimed the girl, as the blood rushed to her face and rose up to the very roots of her hair.

She again attempted to withdraw her hand, but perhaps she did not try very hard. At any rate she did not succeed. 'This is cruel of you! Let me go, please,' she cried, for his arm had stolen round her waist.

'Why should you go, darling?' he asked. 'Stay with me, stay altogether. Be my wife, Edith, my dear little wife. I love you.'

He thought that he was speaking the truth. All fears and doubts had fled when he drew her face to his and covered it with kisses. At the moment he believed that if there had been no duel, no dismissal from his post, no mother even, he would yet have asked Edith Woodall to marry him, would have clasped her in his arms and showered warm kisses on her unresisting lips.

She was at first too surprised to speak, then his kisses frightened her, and then—was she glad? Aye, with a joy that she had never dreamt of, with a gladness far exceeding the timid thoughts of happiness that had sometimes flitted through her girlish brain. Her heart gave a great bound, and for a short while she lay half-unconscious in Ronald's arms. Her head fell on his neck, as he kissed the fair curls and whispered loving words. At last she raised herself by an effort, but not very far—only far enough to look into his eyes and murmur:

'Do you mean it, Ronald? or is it a dream?'

'A dream! no indeed, darling, if you will marry a poor fellow who has not even a home to offer you.'

'Ronald!' she said softly, as the hot blood rushed into her face, 'anywhere with you. Oh! my dearest, I am too happy. Is it true?'

Then she bent over her lover, whose head had fallen back on the sofa as a paroxysm of pain from the wound shot through his whole frame.

'Darling!' she cried. 'Dear Ronald. You are suffering again. What can I do for you?'

'Kiss me,' he said, faintly.

She stooped down and pressed her lips against his.

At the door of the boudoir stood a tall handsome woman with grey hair. She had stepped across the adjoining room noiselessly. A smile of triumph lighted up her fine features as she saw Edith Woodall's first kiss of love. She might have been a tragedy queen, gloating over the destruction of a hated rival—or only a loving mother rejoicing at her son's happiness.

Mrs. Lascelles turned away gently.

'Thank God,' she whispered, 'it is all settled. At last! Thank God!'

CHAPTER XVIII.

AT this Easter-time the hopes of George Stent were realised, and a son was born to him. The Stent horses were once more run off their legs, and their owners were indefatigable in visits of inquiry. Mother and child did as well as could be expected, and there was never a cause for the slightest anxiety. Yet the pale faces of even the male Stents grew paler when they asked the traditional question twice daily, and the traditional answer was welcomed by them with a sigh of relief and returning colour. For although visits at this period in the life of a young married couple are generally paid by the ladies of the family, the interest every Stent took in Clara was such that the men all called at No. 300, Porchester Terrace, on their way to and from the City.

For two whole days Throgmorton Street was without George Stent. Business, however, went on as usual, and neither the Committee of the Stock Exchange nor the Governor of the Bank of England sent round to inquire what was the matter. But, to George, the decision to absent himself on two working days appeared a portentous occurrence. It was early in the morning, in the small hours, that the great event happened, and before the milk came round the whole clan knew it. Some came, and all sent to inquire at once. The news spread rapidly, and was discussed in every Stent household with the tea and toast.

'It is a boy; Clara is getting on very well. But George is not going to the City to-day!'

So ominous did the latter part of this announcement appear to the Stent family, that it formed an absorbing topic of conversation.

'George is not going to the City! Then, after all, there must be something wrong. Clara cannot *really* be getting on as well as they say! Why, when Fred was born, William went to the City as usual! I always thought she was not very strong. Did you notice how worn she looked last Saturday? She did a great deal too much!' and so on.

Events of the same nature were recalled, in order to find a precedent for a Stent not going to his office on such an occasion. But in vain. The Stents always had gone to their offices. A little later perhaps, and not until everything was comfortable at home, but still they had gone. But George had at once, at an early hour, announced to the first inquirers that he was not going to the City. There must be something very unusual to justify such a decision, and not one of the many lady Stents could sit through her breakfast quietly, so anxious were all to rush off to Porchester Terrace and find out what was the matter. But there was nothing the matter. George had broken through old rules, and had shown himself in the light of a ruthless reformer, without any special cause for it. They did not blame him, for one Stent seldom blamed another; they were perfection in each other's eyes. They were surprised at his boldness, and hoped that his business would not suffer in consequence. They attributed this new departure to George's romantic love for his wife. For it had become a dogma in the clan that he idolised Clara—as they expressed it, 'worshipped the very ground she trod on.' Romeo was nothing to him, and love of Leander for his Hero paled in comparison. Therefore they were willing to forgive him, and only hoped that nothing would go wrong in the City. Nothing went wrong, and, notwithstanding his romantic love, George could not bear more than a two days' absence from his daily work. Then he returned to the Stock Exchange, and once more breathed freely. His wife was also relieved, and the nurse was delighted. For during the past forty-eight hours his fussy anxiety and his restlessness had driven her nearly frantic.

Of course Mrs. Lascelles was much rejoiced to hear of her daughter's well-doing and of the birth of a grandchild. But on the whole the news did not create so much excitement in the small family circle at Portino as the intelligence which reached Porchester Terrace very soon afterwards did among the Stents. Little more had been said about Ronald. When two Stents met, they would shake their heads and allude to the young man with sad voices, as if he were indeed a black sheep. At the family gatherings, it was understood that his name should not be mentioned. Occasionally, at long intervals, George was asked in a constrained manner about his

brother-in-law's progress towards recovery. He
answered such questions with a measured coldness
which was understood by the other members of the
class. Then they would all look at each other
significantly, some turning up their eyeballs, some
frowning, some curling the lower lip, but all expressing by intelligible signs, that as they were a reputable Christian family, formal inquiries about the
health of a connection were of course necessary, but
no genuine interest could be taken in a person who
had committed so outrageous an act as to fight a
duel.

But very few days after the birth of the son and
heir—who was to be christened George—a letter
arrived from Portino for Clara. She was of course
upstairs when the postman came, and George Stent
had gone to the City. His instructions were that no
letters were to be given to his wife in his absence.
She must not tire her eyes by reading, nor be excited

by the contents of her correspondence, which might
not be suitable to her condition. Therefore, the day
deliveries were left on the slab in the hall for Mr.
Stent to examine on his return. In the Stent family
it was understood that all the wives opened letters
addressed to their husbands, and all the husbands
those addressed to their wives. That either of them
might have a correspondent who would object to his
or her letters being first read by one of the opposite
sex, was too delicate an idea to enter the head of a
Stent. So George took up the bundle of letters, and
when he had ascertained that his wife was quite well,
proceeded to open them systematically before he went
up to see her. He carefully cut open the envelopes
with a penknife, slowly extracted the contents, and,
after reading them deliberately, placed them on his
left, the unopened ones being on his right. There
were several notes to-day, good wishes from school-
friends who had seen the announcement in the *Times*,

many circulars from shops which supply babies with various requisites, and so on; but there was only one letter from abroad, which George opened last, and began perusing with the same calm deliberation. But, as soon as he had read a few lines, George was fairly startled out of his methodical calmness.

'By Jove!' he exclaimed aloud; 'impossible! Why, it is perfectly absurd!'

He read on, and put the letter down with a fresh expression of surprise.

'That banker must be off his head!' he cried out. 'Surely I must have made some mistake; I will read it again.'

He read again through four closely written pages. This time he could only sit back in his chair and wonder, Could such a thing be?

Soon he rose from his chair and slowly ascended the stairs, still marvelling greatly. He had time to regain some composure before he knocked at the door of his wife's room. After the usual tender inquiries, which he made rather absently, he went into the 'nursery,' as he said, to look at the baby.

' Can Mrs. Stent bear some very surprising news, do you think ?' he said to the nurse.

' What sort of news, sir ? Good or bad ?' asked Mrs. Dutton sharply. She hated Mr. Stent coming to fuss about and fidget, as if she were not able to look after ' her own lady,' and she was always anxious to get rid of him as soon as possible.

' Well, I suppose it is good news,' replied Mr. Stent after some hesitation.

' Then certainly tell her, sir; it will please her and liven her up.'

' But I am not quite sure whether she will be pleased. At least,' he added, with unusual frankness, 'I can't quite make up my mind about it myself.'

' Bless your heart, sir, what is it then ? Queer news,

I should think, if you can't decide whether it's good or bad. My lady must not be upset, but she's very well; and if there's good news from home, it will make her all the stronger.'

'You are quite sure it will not hurt her?' Mr. Stent again asked. 'It is very surprising; she might be startled.'

'Break it gently to her, sir. Tell her you've got some good news for her, and then it won't do no harm,' said Mrs. Dutton, ostentatiously warming some linen at the fire to give Mr. Stent a hint that he might retire. George's last experiment in breaking things gently to his wife had not been brilliantly successful. He still delayed going into her room.

'Shall *I* tell her, sir?' asked Mrs. Dutton, anxious to get rid of him. 'Let me know what it is, and I'll tell it all right, no fear.'

'No, thank you,' replied George, aroused to a sense of his dignity. For the first time he forgot to look at the baby, and to admire its shapeless face and bald head, before returning to his wife.

'There is a letter for you from your mother, Clara,' he said. 'She writes in excellent spirits and sends good news.'

'Oh! I am so glad!' exclaimed Clara. 'What does she say? Read me the letter, George.'

'I know it almost by heart,' he answered, still afraid of startling her too much. 'I can tell you all about it.'

'Do, then!' cried Clara.

'You will be surprised. Don't get excited over it, whatever you do.'

'Please don't worry, George!' said she; 'I am quite well. What is it?'

'But you promise to be calm, Clara. Remember your health and the baby!'

'You will drive me into a fever if you go on like this. Give me the letter!'

'No, you must not hurt your eyes by reading it. Your mother's writing is not very distinct, and she uses thin paper.'

'Then tell me at once, and have done with it. For goodness' sake don't beat about the bush any longer, George,' cried she impatiently.

'Your brother is engaged to be married,' said Mr. Stent, at last obliged to let his rocket off.

'Engaged! To whom?'

'Guess!—to Miss Woodall!'

'To Clara Woodall! Oh, I am so glad, George; she is such a dear creature.'

'So I believe,' said Mr. Stent coldly.

'And I should think it would be a capital match,' added Clara. 'She is well off, I know.'

'It is so good a match that I am quite at a loss to understand it,' replied Mr. Stent.

'Why?' asked Clara. 'Ronald may have been a little imprudent, but he is the dearest, best brother that ever was; and he deserves a very good wife. Oh, I am so glad,' she said again. 'Read me mamma's letter, please.'

Mr. George Stent sat down by his wife's bedside, turned his chair till he got a convenient light, and slowly opened Mrs. Lascelles' letter, while his wife's eyes sparkled with pleasure and impatience. He read very distinctly and deliberately. When he had finished, he replaced the letter in the envelope, and said :

'Now, what do you think, Clara? Is it not extraordinary ?'

'Not at all,' replied she; 'it is quite natural.'

'To me it appears almost incredible !' exclaimed George—'that Mr. Woodall, of Woodalls' Bank, should have consented to his only daughter marrying your brother !'

' George, how can you speak like that ? Our family is quite as good as theirs ! You will make me very angry.'

'I beg your pardon, Clara; I forgot that you were not well. Do not agitate yourself, I beg of you. Still the affair appears to me most singular.'

'She seems to be very fond of Ronald,' said Clara.

'I should have thought that she would be more sensible,' remarked Mr. Stent, who could not repress his ill-humour. 'I made the young lady's acquaintance at Portino, and formed a very high opinion of her.'

'You were right about Edith, George; but you are very unfair to Ronald. You have been vexed with him, poor fellow, ever since that horrid duel.'

'Clara, my dear, how could I do otherwise than disapprove so improper and inhuman an action?'

What was left of the Lascelles' spirit in Clara was now roused, and the discussion threatened to become more acute, perhaps even to develop into a domestic quarrel, when Mrs. Dutton entered the room.

'Now, ma'am,' she said, 'you have been talking quite long enough. It's high time you should be quiet for a bit, or you'll get feverish. You've heard the good nooze' (which Mrs. Dutton had also picked up by judicious listening at the door), 'and you'd better sleep on it for an hour. Please to go downstairs, sir,' she added imperatively to George. He slunk away without another word. In fact he already feared that his expressed dislike to Ronald might have hurt Clara's feelings.

While his wife was confined to her room, George was in the habit of dining in turn with his father and one or other of his brothers. To-day he was going to Mr. Stent senior. By his wife's request, he had left Mrs. Lascelles' letter with the rest of her correspondence, on her table, but he knew every word of the important communication. The servant helped him on with his coat; he gave orders that Mr. John Stent, Mr. William Stent, and Mr. William A. Stent should be informed that he was dining at his father's house, and wished they would come round there after dinner. There was no occasion to write notes. It was so usual for the various members of the family to send for each other, that messages of this description were part of the servants' daily work.

'You look anxious to-night, George,' said his father, while they were eating their soup. 'There is nothing wrong in the City, is there?'

For, of course, long before they had sat down, the inquiries about Clara had been answered satisfactorily.

'Nothing at all,' replied George; 'but I have something to tell you after dinner.'

This answer was sufficient to arouse the curiosity not only of George's father and mother, but also of the servants, and the respectable old butler determined to hear the news as soon as his master. Before the dessert was placed on the table, the clansmen began to assemble. They had all cut their dinners short to respond the sooner to the trumpet-call.

'What have you to tell us, George?' asked the head of the family, as soon as the door was closed on the last arrival. 'Something about young Ronald Lascelles, I suppose?'

'You are right, father,' replied George; 'you will be much surprised.'

'Some new folly, I presume,' said the old man. 'I shall be surprised at nothing that young man does.'

George Stent smiled a thin smile.

'I am quite sure this news will astonish you all exceedingly. You know Woodalls, of course?'

'Woodalls the bankers?' asked Mr. William Stent.

'The same. They have a house in Portino, you remember?'

'Oh yes!' replied Mr. John Stent; 'I met Woodall there when I went to your wedding, George.'

'Precisely; they stand very well in the City, I think,' said George.

'Of course they do,' answered Mr. Stent, senior; 'quite the top of the tree, I should say. They do a great deal of foreign business, now that the Italians are getting on so well. Thoroughly reputable people, and very wealthy.'

'So I have always understood,' said George. 'Rule and Tomkins are their brokers, and I believe that the Woodall orders almost keep them.'

'What has this got to do with young Lascelles?' asked William Stent; 'has he forged a cheque on them?'

'No,' answered George; 'quite the reverse. He is engaged to Edith Woodall, the junior partner's daughter.'

'Good gracious!' came from Mrs. Stent, senior, the only lady present. 'What a lucky young man!'

'Impossible!' cried old Mr. Stent.

'Surely there is some mistake!' suggested John Stent.

'Why, Woodall must be mad!' said William Stent.

'So I think. But the news appears to be true enough. Mrs. Lascelles writes fully to Clara. I have left the letter at home, but I can tell you every word of it. It is too circumstantial to leave any room for doubt.'

'Do you mean to say that Mr. Woodall has consented to allow his daughter to marry that young reprobate?' asked Mr. Stent, senior,

'Not only has he consented,' answered George, 'but he has promised to make Ronald a partner, if a six months' trial in the London Bank should be satisfactory.'

'That is extraordinary! most extraordinary,' said William.

'Not so very curious, after all,' remarked John, after a minute's silence; 'the old man knows that young

Lascelles cannot keep steady for six weeks, much less for six months, and it is a dodge to get rid of him.'

'Ah!' cried George, 'that is quite a revelation to me; possibly that may be the real explanation of the matter. The girl, no doubt, is very much in love with Ronald. It seems that he fought that duel for her sake.'

'And she has been carried away by silly Italian notions,' said Mrs. Stent. 'Not at all surprising; she has no mother, has she?'

'No,' answered George; 'Mrs. Woodall died several years ago.'

'Poor thing! so there was nobody to take care of her, and she fell in love with the first handsome good-for-nothing fellow who paid her attention.'

'But you have not yet told us everything, George,' remarked Mr. Stent, senior. 'Let us hear all about it.'

'It is simple enough. Ronald has proposed to Miss Woodall; she has accepted him, and her father has consented to the engagement. They are not to be married till the autumn, and meanwhile he is to come here and learn banking in Lombard Street. Mrs. Lascelles says that if he likes it after six months, he is to be made a partner directly after the wedding, and will take charge of the Portino house and all the Italian agencies.'

'If he likes it!' repeated Mr. William Stent, with a sneer; 'that means, I suppose, if the London Woodall likes *him*, which is not very probable, I fancy.'

'Not very,' said George, smiling; 'I should think that my respected brother-in-law would be about the last person a London banker would choose as a partner.'

'I should think so, indeed,' remarked John.

'Well, and if the trial should not be satisfactory, what then?' asked Mr. Stent, senior. 'Does Mrs. Lascelles contemplate that contingency also?'

'Oh yes,' replied George; 'it seems to be all cut and

dried. She tells Clara that if her brother does not like the City '—(' Ha, ha !' came from Mr. John Stent, who murmured, ' I wonder how the City will like him !')—' then they are to be married all the same, and Mr. Woodall will make them an allowance.'

' And the young man will do nothing ?' asked William.

' Except gamble and fight duels,' suggested John.

' No,' George answered ; ' in that case Mr. Lascelles will ask for some Government appointment abroad, some vice-consulate or other post, which they will hardly be likely to refuse, as he has some good friends. You see everything seems to have been provided for ; we cannot possibly doubt the correctness of the information.'

' How old is the girl ? She has nothing in her own right, of course ?' asked Mr. Stent, senior.

' She is two-and-twenty, and she has ten thousand pounds of her own,' replied George.

This was the concluding *bouquet* to the fireworks he had let off. Ten thousand pounds, an allowance, and a share in a prosperous bank!—all for that dissipated and foolish young man!

'Some people are very lucky,' observed William.

'Some have to work very hard for years before they can scrape together half of what this young man will get without any trouble,' remarked John.

'What do you think Woodalls make in a year, father?' asked George.

The old man considered the matter for a few moments. 'It is very difficult to tell,' he answered. 'They are doing very well now, and I have never heard of their losing any large amounts since '59, when they had some little trouble for a few months, but nothing to shake them. Edward Woodall, the senior partner, has a fine house at Wimbledon.'

'That is the brother of the Portino Woodall, I suppose?'

'Yes,' continued Mr. Stent; 'his elder brother. The third one died some years ago, leaving a couple of little girls. I think Edward has no children, but he must spend four or five thousand a year at least.'

'Then, at that rate, the firm must be making quite ten thousand?' asked George.

'Much more than that, I should think,' replied Mr. Stent. 'Edward Woodall is not the man to spend all his profits, and I don't suppose he holds more than half share.'

'What a magnificent opening for your brother-in-law!' exclaimed William A. Stent, who had been silent during the greater part of the evening.

'Splendid!' assented George.

'But the young fool will not take advantage of it, said John. 'You may be sure that he will leave the Bank long before the six months are over.'

'I doubt it,' said Mr. Stent, senior; 'I think he is

sharp enough to keep well in with them, at least till he is a partner.'

'It is very likely,' said William A. Stent, who had always had a sneaking weakness for Ronald.

'I am sure he will be quite steady,' Mrs. Stent observed. Ladies, even old ladies, could not be very hard on so good-looking and pleasant a young man.

'Now the question is, what are we to do?' asked George. 'Of course I shall write to congratulate him at once. As he is my brother-in-law, I am obliged to do that much, whether I approve of him or not.'

'Of course,' chimed in the Stent chorus.

'But shall we take him up again?' asked George. 'He will be coming over here shortly, I suppose, and we must make up our minds as to the course to be pursued.'

'We must all write and congratulate,' said Mrs. Stent decisively.

'I do not know about that, mother,' objected John Stent; 'the young man is very reckless, foolish, and extravagant.'

'We can scarcely approve of him yet, can we?' asked William Stent doubtfully.

'But if we do not write, and don't ask him to dinner, and that sort of thing,' said Mr. Stent, senior, 'we shall be putting ourselves all wrong with Woodalls.'

'Let us wait and see how he behaves,' suggested John.

'We can't wait,' declared Mrs. Stent. 'Either we take him up at once, or we drop him for good. Is it not so, George? It will never do to treat him coldly now, and to turn very civil when he is a partner in the Bank. It would look so bad, and make people talk.'

'I cannot drop him,' said George. 'Clara would be vexed.'

'Of course she would. She would have a right to be angry,' assented his mother.

'But it does not follow that we should all congratulate him, and ask him to dinner,' observed John.

'Not at all,' said William. 'He is not *our* brother-in-law.'

'Boys!' exclaimed Mr. Stent, senior, 'do not let us differ about this matter. Remember, though young Lascelles is not a Stent, he is a connection of the Stents. He is about to make a most excellent marriage. George and his wife must, of course, be delighted. In fact we are all very pleased, are we not?'

John and William did not look particularly pleased, but they murmured assent. William A. Stent was genuinely delighted. Mrs. Stent beamed approval on her husband.

'Well,' continued the old man, 'we are bound to be glad that the young man has turned over a new leaf.

Stent and Cowcroft are not so big as Woodalls; and Stent Brothers are a young firm. We must not set ourselves up against the Bank.'

'Certainly not,' echoed his sons and nephew.

'Then let us put a good face upon it,' continued he. 'We will hope that he will become a partner. If he does not, it appears that he will marry Miss Woodall nevertheless, and go abroad. Well, in that case we shall not have lost anything, for we shall be able to drop them easily enough.'

'So we shall!' said the chorus.

'I do not say that *I* would have allowed Ronald Lascelles to marry a daughter of mine,' continued Mr. Stent; 'but, after all, this is Mr. Woodall's business, not mine. If he is good enough for the Bank, he ought to be good enough for Stent and Cowcroft, and for Stent Brothers.'

'True, father.' 'Very true, uncle,' came from different quarters.

'You know, the young man may turn out much better than we expect,' concluded Mr. Stent.

'He may, indeed,' assented George; 'though I hardly dare hope so. But, of course, it is my duty to be cordial to him, and I propose doing my duty to its fullest extent.'

'After all, it was only a youthful error,' observed William A. Stent.

'He has made up for it, certainly, by this excellent marriage,' said John.

'He was very clever to manage it,' remarked William.

'Very,' assented the father. 'Then it is settled. We shall all write to congratulate, and I will call at the Bank to-morrow and wish Mr. Edward Woodall joy.'

'I wish him all happiness,' said William A. Stent.

'So do I,' remarked John.

'I trust they will both be very happy,' observed William.

'I am sure they will,' said Mrs. Stent. 'God bless them !'

Thus was the seal of the Stent approval solemnly affixed to Ronald's engagement.

CHAPTER XIX.

THE BANK.

So warm were the congratulations of all his friends and of many whom he scarcely knew, that Ronald soon believed himself to be the happiest of men. Mr. Woodall was cordial and kind even beyond Mrs. Lascelles' most sanguine hopes. The banker had long felt the want of young and energetic assistance in the business. He was beginning to weary of the details, and to wish to be relieved of much work which no clerk could do and which yet must be done. He had always liked Ronald, and Ronald had done nothing to forfeit his friendship. Of course he might have been better pleased if his daughter had chosen a man of position and property. But such a man might not have fallen in so easily with his views. Ronald was possessed of good abilities; he was a good son, and had grown up, so to say, almost under Mr. Woodall's eyes. He was willing and anxious to work hard, and to work in such a manner as his father-in-law might direct. He had always been popular in Portino, and his duel had made him quite a hero. He understood the ways of the people, and had been used to Italians from his infancy. An English banker, however experienced in the City, would inevitably make some mistakes at first if he had to undertake the conduct of the Portino house. He would not have the patience to spend hours chatting with the voluble natives, even if he possessed the power of conversing fluently in Italian, which was then rarer than it is now. He would certainly offend people by insular stiffness, and possibly be deceived by southern plausibility. Such a man might indeed introduce capital, but the firm was not in want of capital, for Mr. Woodall was too cautious to entertain schemes which he could not control. Therefore, after duly weighing the matter, the banker concluded that any objection he might raise to the engagement would be ill-founded. There was absolutely nothing against Ronald except his want of means, and this would be compensated for by his work and his talents. Besides the points already mentioned in his favour, was the all-important circumstance that Edith loved him very dearly. So much Mr. Woodall knew almost with certainty even before Ronald came to call.

It was on the morning following that first rehearsal that a carriage drew up at the Bank. On the box was the factotum Gasparo by the side of the coachman. Inside were Ronald and Teresina, who had been very willingly pressed into the service, though she knew not why her brother was in such a hurry to go to the Bank. Gasparo inquired whether Mr. Woodall could

receive his young master, and the banker himself came
cut to help the wounded man into his office. Here
Ronald sent Teresina back to wait for him in the
carriage, and at once began by telling Mr. Woodall
that he had proposed to Edith on the previous evening and had been accepted, subject to her father's
consent. This condition had not, however, been
mentioned by the young lady. In her bliss, she had
forgotten all about it. It was an after-thought of
Ronald's own, and a very successful one. The result
of the conversation was eminently satisfactory, as the
reader already knows. Mr. Woodall spoke at once
very cordially. He was glad that the son of his oldest
friend, one to whom he owed more than he could ever
repay, should have been accepted by his dear
daughter. There was no occasion, he said, for Ronald
to tell him of his position and prospects, as of course
he knew all about them. He might possibly have
found a richer man for his daughter, but he could

scarcely have found one whom he himself liked so
well. Ronald might be sure of his consent. As to
the future, he would think matters over, discuss them
with Mr. Lascelles, and then himself come and see
Ronald, who must not imperil his recovery by again
venturing out. Gasparo and Teresina were summoned
to help him back into the carriage, and on their way
Ronald delighted his young sister by telling her that
he was engaged to Edith.

As has appeared from Mrs. Lascelles's letter to
Clara, Mr. Woodall kept his word, and proposed the
handsomest possible arrangements for his daughter.
Charley would of course eventually become a partner,
but he was only fourteen, and Mr. Woodall had no
intention of sending him to Lombard Street for seven
years at least. Mr. Edward Woodall, the elder
brother, was anxious to retire from active business,
and wished Mr. Woodall of Portino to take his place.
Thus, matters could be arranged in the most satis-

factory manner. Both the seniors would leave their capital in the firm, and Mr. Edward Woodall would give up the portion of the profits he had hitherto drawn as payment for his work. Later on, when Charley was old and experienced enough, his father would make a similar concession to him.

The discussion of all these plans, and the charade, which was by no means abandoned, left Ronald very little time for introspection. Edith was an admirable nurse, and now that she could look after him he progressed rapidly. The performance was postponed for a week to allow for more rehearsals, and the number of people invited gradually increased till it included everyone who had ever left a card at the Consulate. It was understood to be a party in honour of Ronald's engagement, and the event created far more interest than engagements generally do. Charley was kept at home three days longer to be able to perform his part. Ronald was able to sit in a steamer chair, and witness the performance from the front row. He was surrounded by friends from very early in the evening, and scarcely ceased shaking hands for a moment. Not till the curtain had fallen amidst loud and general applause did Edith's friends in turn obtain a chance of wishing her joy; for she was stage-manager, and the entrance to the green-room had been carefully guarded by Mrs. Lascelles herself. When at last the guests had all departed, and Ronald had been helped back to his room, he confessed to himself that being engaged was much pleasanter than he had expected.

Another agreeable surprise was prepared for him on the next day: Mr. Woodall called before dinner, and asked to be left alone with Ronald for a few minutes.

'My dear Ronald,' said he, 'I want to ask you a question; you must not be offended.'

'Of course not, sir,' replied the young man ; 'what is it ?'

'I know you have been in London several years, and that your father has not been able to make you as large an allowance as he would have wished. Now tell me frankly, have you not a few unpaid bills and accounts you would like to settle ?'

'To tell you the truth, sir, I have ; but the amount is not large, and as my father has generously offered to continue my allowance for the present, I think that I shall be able to pay them off in less than a year.

'Better settle them at once, Ronald. I will help you. What is the total ?'

'Something under two hundred pounds, sir,' answered Ronald, after a little thought.

'Not more ? are you quite sure ?'

'Quite sure,' replied he, after considering again ; 'rather less, I think. I could tell you exactly in a few minutes.'

'I would prefer to know the exact sum,' said Mr. Woodall; 'I like accuracy.'

'Then, will you be good enough to hand me that desk, sir?' said Ronald. 'I am not allowed to move from the chair yet.'

Mr. Woodall did so, and took up the newspaper while Ronald ran through his bills.

'A hundred and eighty-seven,' said he, after a few minutes.

'There is nothing else?' asked Mr. Woodall.

'Nothing,' answered Ronald.

'Very good. I am glad that you have been so careful; it promises well for the future, my boy. Now, I am going to give you a cheque for three hundred. You will pay me back some day, when you draw larger profits out of the firm than you know what to do with, or you may call it a present, if you like. You are sure to want a little money when you go to London, so just pass me that pen. Thank you. Here you are.'

This was very pleasant; for, to tell the truth, Ronald had been sorely exercised in his mind about the next six months, and about the period which must intervene before he could draw anything from the Bank, even if he were accepted as a partner by Mr. Edward Woodall. Now, with the allowance from his father, he would get on all right till he was married.

A tranquil mind and the best of nursing soon restored him entirely. Before the first hot days of May he could walk about with a stick; and when the Woodalls began to think of moving to their villa in the mountains, he declared himself ready to go to London. Edith did not contemplate his long absence without anxiety. She was too modest, and had too low an opinion of her own attractions, to be absolutely certain of her power over him; on the other hand, she thought Ronald the handsomest, bravest, and best of men, and therefore supposed that every other girl

thought the same. And he had more than once, even
when they were alone together, shown that flippant
humour which she hardly understood and always
disliked. So she not only grieved at the prospective
separation, but feared its consequences.

She need not have been alarmed. Ronald plunged
into the City work with all the energy of which he
was capable, with far more than he had ever displayed
before in anything except sports. His leg was well,
but still weak ; and he could not play cricket, nor ride,
nor walk very much. He arrived when the season
was already well advanced, and he could not walk
about paying visits to remind his old friends of his
existence. So he was invited far less frequently than
in previous years, and he was glad, for it fatigued him
to be obliged to stand about in crowded rooms, when
all the chairs were occupied by ladies, or to sit for
two hours in one position at dinner. In the City he
could move from a chair to a stool, and from the

latter to an arm-chair; for they were very kind at the Bank, and knew of his wound, and Mr. Edward Woodall did everything to make him comfortable. In fact, the two struck up a friendship at once. The sinister prophecies of the Stents were signally falsified. At the first glance he had been inclined to doubt the industry of the handsome young fellow, who came limping into the office dressed in the extreme of fashion, and with a flower in his button-hole; but when he saw that Ronald never took his eyes off the books, nor ceased for a moment to work till the last customer had cleared out and the last rough cash-book was closed, that he was keenly alive to all that went on, and never seemed to weary of learning the details of the business, he rapidly got over his prejudice, which in reality had lived only a few hours. The fact was that Ronald was very determined to master the business, and to think of nothing else till he had done so. He made up his mind that he would not be an ornamental partner. He had hesitated long before proposing to Edith, and he had been afraid of her money influencing his decision. At any rate, Mr. Woodall should find out that he had not made a bad bargain, and that his generosity would be bestowed on a thoroughly deserving object. He would endeavour to earn the money he received from the Bank, so that it might never be said that he was unworthy of a position obtained only because he had married Mr. Woodall's daughter.

With such resolutions, it was not a matter of surprise that he should progress rapidly in the senior partner's favour. Ronald had seen quite enough of London and London life to be able to resist most of the temptations which beset young men when they enter the City; his tastes and character saved him from others, and the only ones to which he was accessible, the attractions of society, hardly tempted him this summer, as he was physically incapable of joining in

many amusements. So there was nothing whatever
to hinder the execution of his resolves. Mr. Woodall
asked him down to Wimbledon from Saturday till
Monday even before he had been in England a week.
He accepted, and found a very comfortable house
surrounded by beautiful gardens. The banker was a
very jovial fellow, and his wife made everyone feel at
home directly. Some other people were stopping
there: a rising barrister and his wife, and one of the
best-known artists of the day. For the house was
full of pictures, and Mr. Woodall devoted all his spare
time and much of his spare money to improving his
collection. Ronald was quite in his element, and the
society he met at Heath Lodge (as Mr. Woodall's
place was modestly called), on this and subsequent
visits, was quite congenial. There was seldom a bore
amongst them; most of the guests were distinguished
in some way, and though the master of the house was
an old man, he remembered what his own tastes had

been in former years, and the younger men had a billiard-room in which they could play or smoke, as long and as often as they liked.

Ronald was not neglected by the Stents. George called at the Bank very soon after his arrival in London. Although everything had turned out so well, there was still a certain sore feeling on both sides on the subject of the Somerset House embassy. Ronald thought that his brother-in-law had been both clumsy and unkind, if not intentionally malicious, while, since the receipt of Mr. Lascelles' letter on the subject, George Stent had had a few misgivings as to whether he had really not exceeded his duty by telling Mr. Charteris about the duel. As a rule, the Stents never repented anything they did, because, as they proudly boasted, they never did anything they could be sorry for. If Ronald had proceeded on the down-hill course the clan prophesied for him after the duel, of course George would have applauded his own wisdom and that of his family. But, as it happened, the contrary had occurred. Ronald had at a bound secured for himself a position which even a Stent might envy, and George was conscious of having strained his duty to abuse a man who might soon be more powerful and more influential (in the Stent City world of course) than himself. This feeling was quickened by a remark of his father's, which showed that the old man either forgot or chose not to remember his own share in the Stent congress.

'You were rather too quick, George,' Stent senior said, ' about going to that official at Somerset House and telling him about the duel. You made a mistake there !'

If the joint and several responsibility of the clan were thus to be destroyed, what remained in the world ? In whom could he then have faith; in whom could he trust ? Was this the rift in the lute, or was it only a little bit of forgetfulness of the old man ?

Probably the latter, as neither he nor any other member of the clan alluded to the matter again. They all agreed to worship the rising sun, and of course George was the first to bow down before the altar—that is, the counter of Woodalls' bank. When he asked for Mr. Lascelles, he quite expected to be shown into a private room and to find his brother-in-law seated comfortably opposite Mr. Edward. Such was not the case. A clerk pointed with his pen towards one of the numerous desks surrounded by ground glass; this particular one was painted 'Bills payable.' George had to knock at the glass himself, as nobody seemed to pay any further attention to him. Ronald popped his head out sideways. Here was an unlooked-for chance to 'sit on' George.

'How do, George?' said Ronald, nodding; 'Clara well?'

'Very well indeed, thank you, and your nephew also,' answered George with studied cordiality. 'Why have you not come to Porchester Terrace?'.

'Bad leg, you know; very busy in the day, and glad to rest in the evening.'

' But you'll come and see your sister soon, won't you ?' asked George, with a sudden and awful fear coming over him. Perhaps, while the Stents had been debating whether they should take Ronald up, Ronald had decided to cut *them !* That would have been carrying the war into the enemy's country with a vengeance. Ronald's answer was not reassuring.

'Oh yes, I'll come some day. Larkins and Co. £243 17s. 4d., did you say ?' turning to his neighbour in the next desk ; 'all right.' Then his head disappeared behind the glass, and he was busy entering figures in his book, as if the Stents did not exist. After waiting for some minutes, during which his anxiety grew intense, George knocked again.

' You will come soon, won't you, Ronald ? Clara is very anxious to see you. Will you dine with us on Thursday ?'

'No, thanks, I'm engaged. Just pass me that bundle of bills, Fletcher' (to his neighbour again), 'thank you. Westropp and Bailey, £52 1s. 6d. on olive oil; I don't see the policy of insurance. Ta-ta, George,' with a condescending nod, when George at last gave it up as a bad job and said 'Good-bye.'

He walked back to 'the House' in a very disturbed frame of mind. Of course he made up his mind that Ronald was not really so busy, and that all this deep absorption in his work was 'put on.' But still the huge room at Woodalls', the wide mahogany counter with its brass edges, the many clerks, the incessant coming and going of customers, the shovelling about of gold as if it were so much dirt—all this, though he had seen it often and often before, made a great impression on him. For hitherto he had been merely one of the crowd, and was glad to have five minutes with the manager and to get away again. But now there was his brother-in-law in the very thick of the work, already initiated, and shortly to become one of those whom merchants asked to see with fear and trembling; who could make or mar a firm by a few words; who held the fates of many old houses in their hands. Every effort must be made to secure him; Ronald must not be allowed to forget the Stents.

CHAPTER XX.

LAST BACHELOR DAYS.

RONALD wrote regularly twice a week to Edith. Here is one of his letters :

> ' 190, Brook Street, Grosvenor Square,
> ' *July 27th*, 186—.

' DEAREST EDITH,

' Many thanks for your charming letter of 20th, which I received yesterday. I am glad you like Bagnuoli. I have not been there since I was a little boy, and almost forget what it is like. All I can remember is scrambling about the rocks and barking my knees dreadfully. I had bare legs in those days. This reminds me to answer your inquiries about mine.

I am getting on very well indeed, thank you, and can now walk steadily for several hours without any pain. Last Saturday I even played croquet at Heath Lodge. But I find it most convenient to have "a leg," and I shall keep up as long as I can; for it gives me an excuse to refuse a lot of invitations to dull dinners. The Stents have made a regular set at me; they seem determined that I should dine with one or other of them every week. This is more than I can stand, so I have pleaded my leg and have got off so far. As people are now leaving town fast, I hope I shall get off altogether. What a blessing that we shall live at Portino and not in London! For if it were otherwise how could we avoid the Stents? And they would soon drive me to Hanwell or to a rupture; both would be disagreeable, but Hanwell would be better than the Stents. Of course, I have seen Clara often. I go there from the Bank, at about five o'clock, when she is generally alone, or at any rate when there is no member of her husband's family about. If there is, I don't go in, having established an understanding with the footman by means of half-crowns. My nephew is healthy, but very ugly—quite a Japanese likeness of his father.

'With your Uncle Edward I get on capitally, and I think he likes me. He is a dear, kind old gentleman, and gets very funny over his bottle of port. He has taught me to like it; but I must not take more than one glass, so he has to get through the rest, which he does not seem to mind. When I dine there he says to your aunt: "Ronald rather likes that '34; we'll treat him to a bottle," and she smiles and says, "Ronald shall have it, certainly;" and then we look at each other and laugh, for the good old soul knows that I only sip one glass, and that your uncle wants it for himself. It is a pious fraud all round. Last week there were a lot of people there, among them Claude Deshamel, whose picture at the Academy has astonished everyone. He is a very clever chap, and as pleasant as he is clever. We made great friends, and I hope he will come to see us at Portino when we have settled down, as he goes to Italy almost every winter. There were some old friends of yours there too—Mr. and Mrs. Bovington; she spoke very nicely of you. It seems that you were at school together—her name was Carson, and she sends you her best love and a number of pretty messages which I have forgotten.

'You ask how I like the work. On the whole, much better than I expected. Very soon I shall have got through the drudgery. I was determined to learn it thoroughly, so I asked your uncle to stick me outside among the clerks, and let me work for a time in all the different places. It was very bewildering at first, as you have to add and subtract and think while people are talking all round you and the doors are swinging incessantly. The continual noise used to worry me, but now I am hardened, and do not not mind it at all. What I have found out is, that I shall not be fit to take charge of the Portino branch in six months. I do not wish to take such a responsibility till I really know the business, and a year at least must elapse before I do. So I hope when a certain event comes off that your father will let me continue my apprenticeship a little longer. Best love to him, and don't forget to remember me to Marietta. Farewell, dear. Many kisses from your loving

' RONALD.'

Except for the last line, this letter might well have been written to a male friend. Ronald felt that he was not writing love-letters; often he even forgot to add the 'many kisses,' and had to put them in a postscript. He could not help it. Edith's letters to him were simple, sweet, and affectionate; but of course she involuntarily took her tone from his own, and expressed

herself with less warmth than she might have done if
he had set her the example. Ronald always felt that he
would be glad if Edith were by his side. He missed
her greatly ; the remembrance of his long talks with her
made him feel the usual London conversation very
flat and wearisome. She had never bored him ; other
people, even pretty girls, often did. He could talk
about anything with her without fear of being
misunderstood ; he could say whatever came upper-
most without being misinterpreted ; but it was as an
intimate friend he missed her, not as if she were his
affianced bride. There was no yearning after her
smile ; no sad recollection of her last words, ; no
hungering after her kiss. So that occasionally he was
exercised in mind, and relapsed into his old doubts. The
relapses were not, however, of long duration. ' Absence
lends enchantment to the view,' and, as time went on,
the blank in his life which only Edith could fill up grew
more and more perceptible. When he heard a good

story, he caught himself saying, 'How this would amuse Edith?' and when he looked at a fine picture he regretted that she was not there to admire its beauties, and enhance his own enjoyment of them. If a dinner-party was particularly pleasant, he regretted that Edith was not in town to join it, and to talk the people over afterwards. At the plays he missed her appreciative criticism, and wished she had been by his side. So he thought that perhaps, after all, he was drifting into the deeper waters of love.

Edith had never cared about anyone before. It was her first experience of love, and therefore she did not know what she ought to expect. Her love for Ronald had grown with her. As a tiny girl, she had teased the tall strong school-boy, had knocked him about unmercifully, pulled his hair, and made him do her bidding; when she was in her teens, she revered him from afar, and was overwhelmed with pleasure when he noticed her: as she grew into womanhood the reverence was exchanged for a more ordinary admiration; but she could never remember the time when Ronald had been indifferent to her. Her affection had not indeed blossomed into a stronger feeling until recent events had hastened its bloom, but it had always existed; and no one of her partners, or of the men who paid her attention, had ever obtained the slightest little morsel of her heart. There were many whom she liked, but she had always liked Ronald much better, even before she loved him. So, though his letters did not quite reach the ideal of what she fancied those of a lover to his betrothed might be, nor to the warmth of those she had seen in novels, she never thought of suspecting Ronald's love. She assumed that he followed the best and most correct examples, and that this was precisely the style in which a clever young man of the world ought to write to the girl of his heart. She soon began to admire them thoroughly. Occasionally there crept over her a slight feeling, not of dislike, but of admiration less warm, when Ronald dropped into the flippant style she knew so well. Never, of course, would she have been so false to her lover as to call him flippant, even to herself. She termed it 'funny.' But she did not like him when he was 'funny,' either in conversation or correspondence, half so well as when he was serious and loving. His narratives were pleasant and chatty, but she sometimes sought some loving words almost unconsciously, and missed them without knowing that there was anything wanting. These were after all but crumpled rose-leaves. For she was thoroughly happy when Ronald's letters told of his continued advance towards perfect health, and of his progress in his work, which, indeed, was fully confirmed by Mr. Edward Woodall's brief notes to her father. So intelligent a young man he had not, said the senior partner, seen for many a day, nor one who worked so hard. Every successive letter confirmed the success of the experiment. She and Mrs. Lascelles had long talks together, and the principal subject of their conversation was, of course, Ronald.

Little did Edith think how his mother had worked to bring about the engagement. Had she suspected the tenor of those many conversations between mother and son, she would almost have sacrificed her love and broken the marriage off at the eleventh hour. But to her, of course, it appeared that things had gone on as usual; that Ronald had somehow—she could not even now tell why or wherefore—fallen in love with her, and had proposed at the earliest opportunity. She was very happy that it was so, and soon grew to adore Mrs. Lascelles in two characters—as Ronald's mother, and as replacing her own whom she had lost.

The wedding was at last definitely fixed for November. Mr. Edward Woodall begged that Ronald might be allowed to return to Lombard

Street after his honeymoon, and spend six or eight months longer in the Bank. Ronald, he said, had mastered all the petty and tiresome details of the outside work and of the books, and could now, if needful, take the place of any one of the clerks or even of the cashier and accountant. But the very assiduity with which he had laboured to learn the mysteries of book-keeping, and checking, and correspondence, and the ways of dealing with the public in daily transactions across the counter, had prevented the senior partner doing what he had intended to do—to introduce him to as many of their customers and friends as possible, to take him on ''Change,' to make him attend in his private room when difficult or ticklish matters had to be discussed and decided; in short, to educate him in the higher branches.

' At present,' wrote Mr. Woodall in October, ' Ronald is already an excellent bank-clerk, and, notwithstanding his short experience, would make a capital cashier or accountant. But he is not a banker at all yet, and before he takes charge of the Portino house I should like to make him one. The business there sometimes requires more than ordinary routine qualities. Difficult questions *may* arise, as they have arisen before, in which consultation with us, who will both be in England, will be impossible even by telegraph. He ought to be able to conduct the affairs of the house without our help, and this is more than we can expect of anyone, however able and industrious, after six months' experience only. Give him another year, and he will be as smart a business man as anyone in England.'

In writing thus Mr. Woodall senior was also expressing Ronald's own views. He wished to be independent, but he did not desire to undertake responsibilities too heavy for his limited experience. He would at Portino be practically the master of a fine business which he had done nothing to build up, and have the supreme control of funds towards which he had contributed nothing. **He felt that** if it had been his own father's bank, **he** would have risked taking charge of matters at once. **If he** made a blunder, and lost a few hundreds, it would only be his father's money, and his father could scold **him for it.** But with his father-in-law's money, **with his** wife's, he desired **to be more** careful. **If he made a** mistake, he knew that his conscience would upbraid him far more sorely than either of the Messrs. Woodall. He wished **to show** himself worthy of the **trust** reposed in him from the very beginning, and to prove **to** both the seniors that they **could** not have done better for themselves than make him **a partner, even if he** had **not** married Edith. Not being very conceited, except, perhaps, about his bowling and his taste in dress, and **judging** his own abilities **very fairly,** he came to **the** conclusion that he required more insight into banking, and a more intimate knowledge **of the** many friends and connections of the Bank, than he had yet obtained, or than he could obtain at Portino. Much as Mr. Charles Woodall desired to return to England, he, of course, gave his consent; and it was arranged that, after spending four weeks in Southern Italy and Sicily, the happy couple should go to London for about a year. From the time of his return to Lombard Street, Ronald was to draw a handsome salary; for, said the two brothers, he will be worth his salt. Thus everything was satisfactorily settled, and, on a foggy evening at the end of October, Ronald left Lombard Street, which he would not re-enter till he was a married man. He was laden with gifts for Edith and himself, for Mr. Edward Woodall had been lavish to extravagance, while the whole Stent family contributed largely, so largely that many of their presents were too bulky to take abroad, and were left in town till the newly married couple had a home in which to place them.

CHAPTER XXI.

THE LAST STRUGGLE.

THERE was plenty of time to think, on the long journey to Portino. The best route was then to Marseilles by train, and thence by steamer. The days were short, and the books Ronald had brought with him did not prove sufficiently interesting for him to spoil his eyes by reading them with the help of a dim railway lamp. There had been hard work in London for the past few weeks, and the severe strain of the past six months had begun to tell on him. He was tired when he got into the train at Charing Cross, and the cold Channel passage and broken night did not refresh him. When in the damp dawn of the autumn, morning he drove from the Northern to the Lyons Railway Station in Paris he was not in the jubilant spirits of the traditional bridegroom. Miserably weary, cold, and depressed, he felt rather as if he were travelling south to a funeral. He passed many hours of the journey to the Mediterranean half waking, half dreaming, but quite wretched. There was no impatience to see his betrothed and to clasp her once more in his arms. Doubts and misgivings again surrounded him, but before they were clearly formulated in his brain he dropped into uneasy slumber. Visions of beauty would appear dimly before him—visions of maidens with dark hair and black eyes, very unlike Edith. Then he would wake with an effort, and strain his eyes and look out of the window on the dreary plains shrouded with autumnal fog. And in a few minutes he would lean back again and wonder what sort of a life would his be, and whether Edith would be happy. She was a dear good creature, and he hoped that he would not make her miserable. But again visions rose before him; this time they took a less ephemeral shape. Lovely Alma Monsell held out her hand to him, and beckoned him to her side. She was dressed in black velvet, with diamonds in her dark hair. He had never seen her thus dressed before. She stretched out a lovely rounded arm half covered with priceless bracelets. Diamonds flashed on her white neck: her bright face was raised towards him; he recognised those arch, dark eyes, the tip-tilted nose, and the tiny mouth which had fascinated him on Ascot Heath. 'Why marry that girl?' she said; 'she is ugly: you will be tired of her soon, and then you will be miserable. She knows nothing of our beautiful large world, and she will tie you to her apron-strings in her narrow one. You can do better. Take my hand, Ronald, come with me!' And she led him away into a region of rosy mists and silver-lined clouds, where they waltzed to the strains of Coote and Tinney's band. Softly and easily they floated round, while his eyes looked into hers, no longer arch, but melting with love. ' A horrid office !' she whispered. ' A City life for *you*, Ronald ? No, you are a bright butterfly, and must not do the work of the ugly ant: stay with me. Here is joy and pleasure; here are brave men and fair women—not money-grubbers and quill-drivers.' Then she seemed to lead him to a great table, all covered with the choicest fruit and flowers, and she held to his lips a sparkling goblet. ' Drink this,' she said ; ' it will cure you : you will be strong again, and merry and happy as before.' And one soft white arm was thrown round his neck coaxing, while the other held up the foaming glass. Then suddenly there was a clap of thunder, and Alma Monsell and the music and the gorgeousness, all collapsed, and Ronald started up ; the porter was shouting : ' *Montereau ! Quinze minutes arrêt.*'

He shook himself, and stretched his cramped limbs.

'This will not do,' he thought; 'those silly dreams worry me. I must keep awake and read, to change the current of my ideas.' And after a cup of coffee, he endeavoured to carry out his resolve. But his eyes were heavy, and his brain exhausted. He could not take any interest in the book; he found himself reading the same sentence over and over again without grasping its meaning. On the other hand, his dream recurred to him again and again, though he was now fully awake. He could not shake off the impression it had made. When at last he gave up trying to keep himself awake, and dropped off into slumber, he had other and worse visions. Edith weeping; his mother upbraiding him for some mysterious crime he had committed, he knew not what; his father turning away his face in anger, while the head cashier at the Bank was holding out a number of cheques for him to sign. Then again the scene on that cold March evening came before him—the steep ascent to the glade near San Cristoforo; the old chestnut tree, with its wide-spreading branches; Della Rocca's huge collar, and a voice calling out to him, ' Do not fight for her; she is a wretched, spiritless creature, quite unworthy of you!' But, while he turned to listen to this strange voice, his adversary fired, and once more he felt the excruciating agony of the bullet in his leg. He awoke with a start: his leg was frightfully painful; the cramped position he was in, the fatigue, and the cold damp had brought back tortures which he supposed were quite at an end. Before he reached Marseilles he was utterly worn out both in body and mind. Piling all the coverings he could find on to his berth, he fell into a sleep as soon as he got on board the Messageries boat. But his sleep was not of long duration : the mistral blew hard, and the steamer pitched violently; the motion was too severe for anyone to be comfortable in a berth; the voyage of thirty-six hours was as tiring as the land journey had been. But Ronald had made up his mind as to the course he would pursue.

The wind had diminished in force before they reached Portino. The stars were beginning to appear in the dark sky when the passengers were put ashore. On the quay stood Mr. Lascelles. Ronald was relieved not to see his mother; the Consul was shocked to find that his son could not get ashore without assistance. By the flickering and uncertain light of the gas lamps he could not see Ronald's face distinctly, but he appeared wan and tired.

'Your mother and Edith are at the house, Ronald,' said the Consul; 'they are getting tea ready for you, and dinner as well, so that you may have your choice. I thought they had much better not come down to the quay this nasty cold evening. They might have caught their deaths waiting about for that wretched steamer! What a dreadful voyage you must have had! She was due at noon, and Edith was looking out for her through our telescope all day. I have sent for a carriage, Ronald,' he continued; 'I am sorry to see you can't walk yet.'

'Only the cold and stiffness of the journey,' answered the young man. 'I have been quite well for months. I believe this will go off in a day or two.'

'I hope so, indeed, in time for the wedding. Now get in and let us be off home. Cataldi will look after your luggage. Give him the ticket.'

Ronald was silent during the short drive. At the Consulate, Teresina rushed to the porte-cochère to meet them, while Mrs. Lascelles and Edith came forward in the entrance hall. He kissed them all, and was dragged into the bright warm dining-room, where his sister began removing his wraps.

'How pale you are, dear!' exclaimed Mrs. Lascelles.

'Dreadful!' cried Teresina. 'You look like a corpse, Ronald. What is the matter?'

'I am very tired,' answered he, sinking into an armchair; 'and my leg hurts again.'

'You look very worried and worn out, dear Ronald,' said Edith, bending over him. 'We shall be too much for you to-night.'

Instinctively she guessed what was passing in his tired brain. These greetings and inquiries were overwhelming him just then. He yearned for rest—entire rest. Their affection annoyed him; but he kissed Edith's forehead.

'You are all too good,' he said. 'I will have some tea, if you please, and shall go to bed early.'

There was a hush of disappointment all round. Teresina had looked forward to this evening as to a particularly festive occasion. Mr. and Mrs. Lascelles had expected to see their son come back in good health and full of spirits. As to Edith, she had been picturing the return of her hero for weeks past. She had expected him to fly first to her and take her in his arms. Then he would greet his mother and sister, and would tell all about his life in London, and her uncle and his friends, and they would spend a very, very happy evening. Her father was coming in later, and Stornello and Donati were impatient to see their old ally. Instead of Ronald flying to embrace her, he limped slowly forward, leaning on his stick and on Teresina's arm. Instead of the light of love in his eyes, she saw them drooping and lifeless. No cheery smile brightened his face, which was drawn and anxious. He had not the inclination, or lacked the power, to ask questions, and his silence prevented them asking any.

The tea was brought in, and Teresina placed a little table by his side. He refused to eat, and begged them to have their dinner as usual. As usual! How could they sit down to the festive viands which had been prepared, while he for whom they had waited so hopefully was lying silently in an armchair, unable or unwilling to join them ?

'You are tired out, my boy,' said Mr. Lascelles; 'you want a good night's rest.'

'I do, indeed,' said Ronald quietly; 'forgive me for not being able to talk.'

They were all very affectionate and good, and he was at home; but it appeared to him that the visions of the past three days were more real than his present surroundings. He felt cross with them all, somehow, and had trouble to conceal his irritation.

'I will look after the fire in your room,' said Mrs. Lascelles, rising.

'Thank you, mother. Edith,' he said, 'will you come near and sit down by me for a moment?'

Edith obeyed, while Mr. Lascelles and Teresina discreetly began talking about the weather, and, drawing one of the curtains, looked out into the starlight night.

'Do not be angry with me, dear child,' he said to his betrothed; 'forgive me, whatever may happen; I am not well.'

'There is nothing to forgive,' answered she; 'you are completely done up by your journey. You ought to have stopped a couple of days at Marseilles to rest, and have come on by the next boat.'

'I have something for you,' continued Ronald, trying to get at his pocket, 'something from myself, and no end of things from your uncle and all your folks.'

'Oh! never mind them now, darling,' said Edith almost with tears in her eyes. 'I am in no hurry: to-morrow will do. I am only so very sorry that you have knocked yourself up by hurrying so for my sake. You are always injuring yourself for me. I wish I could do something to deserve it.'

'Who knows?' answered Ronald gently; 'your affection may be put to a very severe test. Try to think well of me, whatever happens.'

Edith was alarmed at the solemnity of his tone ; but before she could answer Mrs. Lascelles came in.

'Your room is warm and comfortable, Ronald,' said she ; 'and your bag is upstairs.'

'Then, if you will allow me, I will go at once. I am not fit for anything to-night, and will leave you to your dinner. Teresina, will you give me your arm ? Good-night, Edith dear. Father, would you mind coming upstairs to me for a few minutes when you have done dinner ?'

'Will not to-morrow do, if you have anything to tell me, Ronald ?'

'No ; to-night, please. I shall be better by-and-by, when I have had a bath ; and send me some more tea, please, mother.'

An hour later Ronald was lying on the couch he had hoped never to require again. A warm bath had reduced the pain, and his feeling of impatient irritation had diminished.

'Father,' he said, when Mr. Lascelles entered, 'after all, I can't marry Edith.'

'Good heavens, Ronald!' exclaimed the old gentleman, 'what has happened?'

'Nothing, father, except that I am sure I do not love her.'

'Nonsense, my boy; you are tired and out of sorts. Go to bed, sleep soundly, and you will wake up more in love with her than ever.'

'No, father,' replied Ronald; 'it has taken me a long time to find out, but I am now quite sure. I like the girl very much; she is everything I could wish for; but I don't love her.'

'You have taken a fancy to some one else while you were alone in London, Ronald.'

'No indeed, I have not fallen in love with any one, upon my honour. But I have discovered that I shall never be happy with Edith, and shall never be able to make her happy.'

‘Ridiculous !’ exclaimed Mr. Lascelles ; ‘it is positively absurd to come at the eleventh hour with such
a fanciful theory. You should have thought of all
that before. We talked it over six months ago, and
you made up your mind then that you were very fond
of her; and so you are now, only something has put
you out.’

‘It is of no use, father. I was wrong to propose to
her—very wrong. But, fortunately, I have found out
my mistake just in time.’

‘No, Ronald ; if it is a mistake, it is too late to
remedy it. You must go on now.’

‘I shall break it off to-morrow morning. That is
why I wanted to see you to-night.’

‘You cannot break it off,’ said Mr. Lascelles.
‘Things have gone much too far. Think of the
scandal !’

‘I cannot help the scandal,’ answered Ronald.

‘But you are surely not so selfish as to make a

number of people who love you miserable for the sake of an idle fancy,' exclaimed the Consul. 'Believe me, my boy, this is a delusion of yours. You and Edith will be happy as the day is long.'

'It is no delusion, father,' repeated Ronald: 'it is the bare, terrible truth.'

'Even if it were,' replied Mr. Lascelles, 'which, mind, I do not admit for a moment, you have no right to back out now. You would make the girl wretched; you would destroy her life.'

At this moment Mrs. Lascelles entered the room. 'What are you talking about?' she asked. 'Ronald ought to go to bed. He is quite done up; and all the talking can be done to-morrow.'

In a few words Mr. Lascelles told her what the matter was. Meanwhile Ronald lay quietly on his couch, and merely nodded when his father concluded.

'My dear boy,' exclaimed Mrs. Lascelles, 'your hard work in London and your journey must have upset you. Go to bed, and do not let us hear anymore about it.'

'Mother, I cannot drop the matter like that; my mind is made up. I shall break off the engagement to-morrow.'

'You would break dear Edith's heart,' said Mrs. Lascelles.

'Oh, no; girls' hearts are not so easily broken. She will cry a little bit, and be sad for a week or two. Next year she will marry some one else.'

'You do her great injustice,' said his father angrily, ' I really begin to believe that you are right, and that you don't deserve such a thoroughly good, affectionate girl, who loves you as if you were the only man in the world, while you shilly-shally like a silly baby.'

'Don't get angry with him,' exclaimed Mrs. Lascelles, as she noticed an ominous flush on Ronald's cheeks. ' He is not well, and you must make allowance for him.'

'I do not wish any allowance to be made for

me!' cried Ronald. ' Is it better to marry her and make her miserable for ever than to tell her frankly that I cannot love her, and hope that she will console herself with some one else by-and-by?'

'You beg the question,' said the Consul.

'You would not make her miserable,' said Mrs. Lascelles. 'If I thought so for a moment, I would prevent the marriage myself. We know you better than you know yourself. Think of the grief you would cause all who love you; and how about the arrangements with the Bank and Mr. Woodall?'

'Of course they would be at an end,' answered Ronald. 'But it is not difficult to find men much more able than myself, who would willingly join Woodalls' Bank and bring in money as well.'

'Perhaps not,' replied his father. 'But neither Edward Woodall nor his brother have found one, though they have been looking for some time. You seem to suit them thoroughly.'

' You would surely not have me marry against my inclinations to please the brothers Woodall, father ?'

' No, my boy; certainly not. This is only one, and certainly the weakest, of the many reasons against your breaking off the match.'

' It is madness to think of it,' observed his mother. ' What would you propose doing, Ronald ?'

' Returning to England at once ; I shall then look about for an opportunity to emigrate. Australia would suit me well, I think.'

' The notion of going twelve thousand miles away to avoid an excellent marriage !' exclaimed the Consul.

' What should *we* do ?' asked Mrs. Lascelles gravely.

' You, mother ? why nothing, of course. You would go on as usual.'

' Do you think your father and I could ever hold up our heads in Portino again ?' asked Mrs. Lascelles gently. ' Just consider the matter, Ronald. Your father would be estranged from his oldest and dearest friend; I should lose one who has become as dear to me as a daughter. We are all under obligations to the Woodalls. We should both be cut off from the society which makes this place tolerable to us. Even poor Teresina would be injured; she would be deprived of many little pleasures, and surely she has not too many as it is. The Woodalls would be plunged in misery and grief, which they would attribute to us; and we should practically be shut out from everything, and be worse than strangers in the town. And to make up for this great trouble and all the small worries which must follow, we should know nothing of our only son, except that he was sheep-farming or digging somewhere at the antipodes.'

This was the first argument which touched Ronald at all. He was moved, and his face showed it. His mother continued:

'You would ruin the life of a faithful girl—for
indeed, my boy, I know her character; you would
destroy the happiness of your parents, who love you
more than anything in the world; you would deeply
grieve two most worthy men who have trusted you
and heaped favours on you; you would break your
own sacred word; and you would destroy your
prospects—all for what? For an idle, silly fancy, the
result of your being too much alone, and having over-
worked yourself. My dear Ronald, you could not do
it; you would not do it; you shall not do it!'

A mortal fear seized the poor mother lest her
beloved son should thus wreck all their hopes at the
moment of fulfilment. She burst into tears, and,
covering her face with her handkerchief, sobbed
piteously.

'My boy,' said Mr. Lascelles, rising, and placing a
hand on his son's shoulder, 'look at your mother's
grief, and stick to your determination if you dare.

You call it conscientiousness; *I* should term it obstinate folly. You place your idle fancies above the wisdom and experience of your parents! They know better what is for your happiness than you do yourself. Heaven knows I have been a lenient father to you. I have never exerted my paternal authority before, but I do so now. Break your mother's heart, break that poor girl's heart, break your sacred word of honour, at your peril! If you do, you are no son of mine!"

The Consul's voice was choked with emotion. He remained standing, his eyes fixed on Ronald, while a single tear coursed slowly down his wrinkled face. Before such an appeal no son could remain unmoved, even had he possessed a harder heart than Ronald's. The young man was much exhausted and in pain. Whatever the result, it could not be right to cause this grief to his parents, and bring a father's curse on his head. Himself sobbing, he held out his hand.

'Stop, father,' he cried, in a broken voice; 'do not cry, mother dear: I will do as you wish. It is settled for good or for evil. God grant that you may be right!'

CHAPTER XXII.

THE CHAPEL AT PORTINO.

THE battle was over, and the defeated one sought his couch, weary and exhausted. No visions disturbed him. The deep dreamless sleep of complete prostration came to soothe his excited brain. When he at last awoke, it was nearly mid-day. Strict orders had been given that he should not be disturbed, and they were rigidly observed. He lay idly for some time before he rang his bell. At first the events of the previous night seemed to be only a dream, but gradually they came back clear and distinct to his memory. He had done what he thought his duty. It had been his duty to place the matter

clearly before his parents; he had thought it his
duty to break the marriage off. They disagreed with
him; they considered that it would be foolish, wicked,
and dishonourable to do so. He must bow to their
opinion, and there should now be no further doubts,
no more hesitation. He would do his best to make
Edith happy, and would no longer give way to idle
dreams and fancies. Possibly he would soon learn to
love her, since she possessed every lovable quality,
except that unfortunate nose! Probably he would
soon cease to notice the nose, and would be as
fond of her six months hence as any husband
could be. The prospect was so pleasant, the future
looked so bright, that he felt he would have been
indeed a fool to sacrifice himself and her on account
of exaggerated scruples. They should never trouble
him more. He would make her a good husband, and
his father and mother would be blessed in their
children and grandchildren.

Then he rang the bell, and, when he rose, found
that he could use his limbs again as usual. But his
mother sent for Dr. Salviati, who said that the damp
and cold had brought on a neuralgic attack, and that
Ronald must be careful for a year or two, and keep
the injured leg warm. So the alarm of the family
subsided, and everything went on smoothly hence-
forward. There was only a week to the wedding, and
the week passed quickly and pleasantly. The tiny
English church was full of people. Not only the
English colony and all Ronald's Italian friends, but
many others — customers of the Bank, merchant
captains, mates of vessels which frequented Portino,
Marietta with her brothers and nephews and nieces,
Gasparo and all his family, the odd man who helped
occasionally when Mrs. Lascelles gave a party, the
two *huissiers* of the Bank with their belongings,
the messengers and porters with their wives and
children, the clerks and the mothers and aunts of

the clerks, Cataldi—the old factotum of the Consulate
—with a whole tribe of Cataldis, the pastrycook, the
butcher, and the fruiterer, who supplied the Palazzo
Woodall—in short, nearly all Portino—crowded the
place of worship and overflowed on the Piazzetta in
front. All were eager to see their beloved signorina,
the rich English heiress, who had become quite one of
themselves, married to the gallant youth who had
fought for her, had suffered for her, and had gained
the prize he so richly deserved. In his way he, too,
was as popular as Edith. No one could handle a boat
as well as the signorino handled the *Santa Lucia.*
When he started in a rowing match, none could scull
like him; he wore down his opponents and won
easily whenever he liked. He talked to the fishermen
in their own dialect, and was not a bit proud. He and
his little sister (*che bellina!* to be sure) used to come
out on the Riva and get them to sing, and he would
lend a hand himself at hauling in the nets. He had

gone round with a collecting-book for poor Giambattista, when the boat capsized, and was lost in that
violent scirocco, and the owner was only saved by the
special intercession of the Virgin. The English
signorino had collected five hundred francs, and
Giambattista got a beautiful new boat. And they
remembered the dark days of smoke and tumult,
when innocent citizens and poor peasants were
seized by the soldiers, and Ronald had saved a
lot of them by opening the back door of the
Consulate, and affording them the protection of
the British flag. He had gone out and spoken to
the Royalist colonel, and had refused to give them
up, and had dared the officer to come and seize them.
And in the hospitals, who had brought the wounded
soup, and meat, and fruit, and flowers, but la signorina
Woodall? So there was an assemblage as numerous
as, and more enthusiastic than, if the wedding had been
that of a Sforza to a Colonna. There were loud shouts

of *Evviva!* when Mr. and Mrs. Lascelles and their son
drove up. When the bride entered the doors, on the
arm of her father, they were still louder, and the crowd
pushed up behind her into the church till every inch
of standing-room was occupied.

Ronald looked pale and preoccupied. He had dismissed his doubts for ever, but he felt the solemnity
of the occasion. But the bride was radiant. Proud
of her husband, who was to her the ideal of all that
was noble and manly, she looked up at him with eyes
full of sweet love and tenderness. She answered in a
voice far clearer and firmer than his own ; and when
the ceremony was over, and the happy couple were
receiving congratulations in the vestry, many noticed
that while she looked bright and almost exultant,
the bridegroom was silent and *distrait*. 'White
certainly does not suit her,' thought he, when Edith
raised her veil. It was a good thing she had not
cried, for otherwise her nose would have been red.

But she must not wear white in future. There was a want of colour about her altogether ; she required blue or pink to liven her up. On the whole, however, she looked nice—quite as nice as he could expect. What ought he to say on their way back from church to her home ? Ought he to talk of their future happiness, and rave about her beauty ? Or would it suffice if he alluded to the weather, which was indeed brilliant ? But he need not have been anxious on the subject, for the enthusiastic crowd prevented his having to invent conversation. The *Evvivas* did not cease. Hats and caps were thrown into the air, handkerchiefs waved, and people pressed round the brougham to wish them all happiness. The coachman could not have forced his way through, if Ronald had not himself put his head out, and said : '*Grazie tanti, amici, ma preglo! lasciate passar la carozza, la moglie la già fame. Le nozze danno appetito !* This joke was quite within the capacity of the spectators. It tickled the people vastly to hear Ronald talk glibly of his *moglie*, and to suggest that she was hungry. A lane opened for them through the crowd, and they drove away rapidly, followed of course by dozens of ragged boys to whom the bridegroom must give largesse.

The presents were set out in the drawing-room at the Palazzo Woodall, and people admired and grew quite enthusiastic over them. Ronald had been brought up in a simple way, and many of the little luxuries to which young men are now accustomed were unknown in the Portino Consulate. He did not seem to care very much for asparagus-tongs and sugar-sifters and silver-gilt salt-cellars and fish-knives. The interest they aroused in him was languid. From an artistic point of view, they were not very beautiful; and as to their usefulness, he failed to see it. Asparagus tongs are awkward to handle, and Ronald generally took them in his left hand while he helped himself to asparagus with his right. Of course silver

salt-cellars were very nice, but glass ones answered
the purpose as well. As to fish-knives, they were
only just 'coming in,' and the old-fashioned fish-
'slice' which figured among the presents, was just
about the clumsiest tool ever invented in an age
desirous of display. Ronald stood in a corner of the
room, listening absently to the friendly talk of
Stornello and Donati, briefly answering Colonel
Martini's hearty speeches, and watching Edith, who
floated about like a sylph from one friend to another,
talked with everyone, smiling and blushing, and
herself appreciating very highly the gifts that had
been lavished on her. No one could look at her and
not see that to her this was indeed the happiest day of
her life. Not the tiniest cloud disturbed the serenity of
her mind; her fresh young heart, full of love for her
husband and gratitude to Heaven, was brimful of joy
which sparkled on her fair face. Teresina darted hither
and hither, lively, gushing, and in overwhelming spirits,

chattering to one in Italian, to another in English, leaving her sentences half finished and flying from one friend to greet another. Charley walked about solemnly in the glories of a new black cloth suit, and with a bouquet of orange flowers in the button-hole of his Eton jacket. He deigned to approve of his sister's choice, and to consider Ronald 'a regular brick, you know—a sort of Quentin Durward,' being just then full of Scott's novels. Mrs. Lascelles was radiant, and not a shadow crossed her handsome face. No recollections of that last battle with her son troubled her. The two fathers talked with a group of elderly men, a few of the numerous friends a long and honourable career had gained for both. A smile of paternal pride would light up Mr. Woodall's face when the happy bride passed near him—and she never did so without a glance of affection for her father. Mr. Lascelles looked towards his son with a little anxiety ; but Ronald's appearance did not betray

the acute boredom from which he was suffering.
How he wished that all this were over ! How tired he
was of being congratulated and told that he was the
luckiest fellow alive, and having his hand pressed,
and hearing that he was the envy of all Portino ! He
raised his eyes, and looked out of the window. There,
on the still waters of the harbour, was the *Santa Lucia*,
her tall taper mast and long hull catching his eye at
once among the clumsy trading-vessels and low
feluccas by which she was surrounded. She was gaily
dressed in bunting ; from the topmasthead to the
bowsprit and boom-ends stretched halliards carrying
flags of all colours which were flying out in the soft
breeze. How he wished he could throw off that blue
frock-coat, specially ordered for the wedding, and
draw on the snug jersey, and rush off to the Molo,
and feel the sea breeze cooling his face, and sail away
altogether from all these good, kind, but terribly tiresome people !

Sail away? With whom? Only with Gasparo.
As he stared vacantly over the bobbing heads of his
friends, and watched the sea-birds skimming over the
sparkling water, no visions rose before him of sailing
across summer seas with his fair bride. He had not
yet realised that she was his, and that his life was
henceforth to be spent by her side. That graceful
figure floating about in Brussels lace and tulle was
not yet a part of his existence. He forgot her completely, as his thoughts flew back to stormy evenings,
when he and Gasparo had struggled with the huge
mainsail flapping in the wind, and had fought hard to
deprive the storm of its prey; when he peered into.the
darkness, brightened only by the foam of the waves ;
when they had worked the good little ship through the
narrow inner passage, while the wind drove the spray
in blinding sheets over them, and that Gasparo was
peering out to windward, yearning for a glimpse of
the light on the Molo. There was joy in these fights

with the elements, though there had been discomfort and wretchedness at the time : the wet clothes, the keen wind, the hunger, and the cold were forgotten. Now he remembered only the triumph of having brought the *Santa Lucia* home in the teeth of a wild tramontana, of having safely weathered all the rocks and cruel reefs, and sailed into the quiet anchorage without the loss of a spar or a rope. Then he recollected their trip to Ischia, when Stornello and he started for a week's cruise, and how the yacht had run for twenty miles heeling over before a quartering breeze alongside of a passenger steamer. Her captain had ordered them to fire up, and great clouds of smoke issued from her funnel and stained the blue sky, but it was in vain. The *Santa Lucia*, cleaving the tiny wavelets and heeling to under a cloud of canvas till the water washed up her decks to the skylights, had sailed out of the black cloud of smoke and soon left the ugly puffing steamboat far astern. How Gasparo had laughed and cheered, and chaffed the people on the steamer! Then Stornello and he had opened a bottle of Falerno, and drunk the healths of the passengers on the packet. And Stornello, raising his glass in one hand, had dropped it as the *Santa Lucia* gave a lurch, and the sweet Falernian went down into the salt sea.

Ronald started. A soft hand was laid on his arm.

'They are waiting for us to go down to breakfast, Ronald dear,' said his wife.

CHAPTER XXIII.

SICILIAN DAYS.

RONALD determined to dismiss for ever his idle dreams, weak doubts, and morbid self-communings. His work and his duty in life were clear, nor was his path a thorny one. Nay, rather was it strewn with roses. If the roses were not exactly the variety he would have selected, that was surely a very insufficient reason for sickly repining. The course before him was now plain and withal far easier than he had any right to expect. He would have wished to go to work again at once and enter seriously on the career of which he had so far only fringed the border. The honeymoon in Sicily, that strange southern land full of fascination and contrasts of wild grandeur and soft beauty, was not the remedy he required to restore tone to his mind. He wanted bracing up by manly work, by contact with hard practical men who had not wasted hours and days in vain wishes and foolish introspection.

With Edith only as his companion, travelling for pleasure through lovely scenes, he felt that he had too much time on his hands, too little to occupy his thoughts. In the honeymoon newly married people are supposed to have enough to do to please each other: according to tradition, they do not require any other occupation. Even when they look at water-falls, or climb up mountains, or visit churches, they are understood to be so taken up with each other as not to care very much whether the waterfall is a humbug, the view shrouded in mist, or the church a tawdry bit of restoration. This is an opinion largely entertained, if not quite universal. But, notwithstanding his resolute efforts, Ronald found that he could not conform to tradition. Edith was, indeed, perfectly contented and happy. To lean gently on his arm, to look up lovingly into his face, and to find there a responsive smile, seemed to her all she required. She enjoyed the beauties of nature and art keenly, and her joy was intensified by the presence of her hero by her side. It was a matter of course, an absolute dogma to her, as true as her own existence, that Ronald loved her far more than in her own opinion she deserved, and that dogma alone would have sufficed to make her happy during these first weeks, even had they been spent in the Desert of Sahara. The inconveniences of travelling about in Sicily were new and amusing to her, and every little discomfort or delay became to her a source of fresh enjoyment.

Knowing Italian as she did, she very soon learned to

understand the dialect, and what would have ruffled the feathers of a London beauty, in her only caused a bright laugh.   What did it matter if they found nothing but sour bread and nasty cheese at an inn which had been vaunted to them as the best in the district, as the very place for English people of quality to stop at ?   She would explore the village and talk to the people, amusing and pleasing them ; and she would find eggs, and coax an old woman to sell her a skinny fowl, and make Ronald carry her treasures back to the inn, and after all they would sit down to a sufficient meal.   Of course the breast of the fowl —the only portion any ordinary jaws could chew— would be for Ronald.   She was not very hungry, oh no ! a couple of eggs were enough for her !   Again, when the harness gave way, and their carriage was stuck on a desolate hill-side, miles away from any town, with the early twilight of November approaching rapidly, she was not alarmed at having to trudge for hours through mud and mire. Ronald was by her side, and she felt no fatigue.

The wife of the English Consul at Palermo had suggested that they ought to ask for an escort of *carabinieri*, as brigands were about. Edith only looked at Ronald and smiled. He had a revolver which he wore round his waist, and with him she was not afraid of a dozen brigands. Perhaps her bright face, her good humour, and her friendly ways really protected them from attack. At any rate, they were never molested, though they heard of other travellers in the neighbourhood being plundered of all their belongings.

The handsome couple soon became popular all round Palermo. In the eyes of the swarthy Sicilians, Edith was the ideal of beauty. They cared not for her mouth being too large, nor did they measure the length of her nose by the standard of the Medicean Venus. She had fair hair, blue eyes, and a white

and pink complexion, and that was enough to make
her an angel to them. Every little incident of
the trip was a new cause of pleasure to Edith,
because every incident, in her opinion, brought
out the great and good qualities of Ronald, *her
husband.* Edith was not spoiled, nor was she
exacting. Ronald resolutely determined to be in
love with his wife, and he acted up to his resolution.
He paid her much deferential attention, and very
small attentions from him went a long way. Gentle,
thoughtful, and kind he had always been with her, as
with all women; for there was in him an inborn
gallantry which prevented his behaving otherwise
to the ugliest and oldest of her sex. But he now
made strenuous efforts to be more than merely
attentive to all her wants; he endeavoured to do
better even than to anticipate her slightest wishes.
He became loving and devoted. He taught himself
to carry out, in all its details, the unwritten rules

which guide a passionate lover. If he helped her
into the carriage, he gave her hand a slight but
significant pressure. When she was getting out, he
lifted her down in his arms, instead of merely assist-
ing her in the ordinary manner. If she handed him
anything, he stooped and kissed her hand before
taking it. When she joined him, ready for a walk,
and placed her arm in his, he never forgot to kiss
her on both eyes. When she sat by him, he would
gently stroke her fair hair. At every caress, Edith
would blush and look at him lovingly in return.
When, after dinner, they could manage to make
themselves comfortable (which was not always the
case), he would make her take the nicest arm-
chair he could find, and lie down on a rug at her
feet, looking up into her eyes.

Soon all these attentions grew easy and natural
enough. Gazing into those soft blue orbs, whose
glance was always gentle and loving, Ronald's resolve

to cherish and guard the sweet girl who trusted him so implicitly was daily strengthened. Her heart, her thoughts, her whole life, were so entirely his, she leant on him with such confidence, turned to him with such thorough trust, looked up to him with such devotion, that no man, not in love with another woman, could have done otherwise than return something at least of her affection. Aye, but how much ? Ronald strove gallantly to give her back all she gave ; to abandon his heart to her keeping, as she had abandoned hers, to see in her his own true helpmate and companion, to weave her image into all his future hopes and aspirations. He would at once begin to tell her of his work and of his past difficulties, so that he might get used to confiding in her and consulting her. And when he carried out this resolve, he found in Edith an intelligent and sympathising listener. She had not been at the head of her father's household for seven years without profiting

by her position. She was no silly boarding-school
miss, ignorant of everything, polished with a super-
ficial veneer, gathered from lesson-books. Of the
world, the fashionable world, she certainly knew
nothing. The gossip of society papers, the slang
of what are known as the upper circles, were un-
intelligible to her. But she knew something of
politics, and she had strong sympathies with Italy
and Italian aspirations. Of the complicated machinery
by which the business of the world is carried on, of
trade, shipping, banking, and finance, she understood
more than many men. Such terms as discount,
bills, policies of insurance, freights and shipping
charges had been household words to her since
her childhood. She had often helped Mr. Woodall
with his correspondence during his brief annual
holiday at Bagnuoli. The more important letters
were sent up to him by a mounted messenger, and
Edith often wrote the replies to his dictation. She

knew every one of the staff at Portino, and also some of the clerks who were now in London, for they had spent a year or two in Italy first. Nearly all the Italian agents had come down to Portino, and had been invited to the Palazzo Woodall at one time or another.

So Ronald discovered, to his surprise, that he had very little to teach his wife. She knew nearly as much as he did himself about the routine of banking, and much more than he did about the Italian affairs of the firm. The discovery came on him as a surprise, for Edith was above all womanly, and had never brought out her knowledge of business, nor exhibited her acquaintance with matters which are generally supposed to be understanded of men only. Her father and the chief cashier were probably the only male persons who were aware that she knew more than most people of either sex. Her gentle ways and unassuming modesty were quite incompatible with the accepted

type of the superior woman. Even her affianced lover
had not guessed that she was, in this respect, so
different from other girls. He had, therefore, never
alluded to business matters except casually and in a
general way, and she had abstained from introducing
a subject which Ronald had not thought proper to
discuss with her.

Now she was pleased to be told of the London office, of the business carried on there, of the
rush and hurry of the great city. She loved
to hear Ronald tell of the doors swinging incessantly
on their hinges, the tellers and cashiers in their glass
cases, the ways of their great customers, so different
from the Italian indolence, the rapidity with which
huge transactions were proposed, accepted or declined,
and carried out, of the people who came to see her
uncle, of the merchants, noble lords, country squires,
and money-lenders who elbowed each other in the
front of the long counter. And her heart swelled with

joy at the thought that she was the humble instrument by which her own Ronald should be rewarded for his devotion and heroism—should occupy a place worthy of him, as the chief to direct and control this great house—the man who would receive merchant princes and Peers of the Realm as their equal if not their superior.

If she had been filled with sweet thoughts of happiness and love when he lay at her feet and kissed her hands, or when he lifted her tenderly and clasped her in his strong arms, her heart overflowed with pride now that he trusted her with his plans, and with those details of his work which would have been dry and repellant to an ordinary woman. What, she often thought, had she done to deserve such ineffable bliss?

Ronald was so handsome and so manly that his very appearance made all look at him; so brave that he had thought nothing of risking his life for her, so good and loving that her every wish was anticipated before she could express it, so thoughtful that every crumpled rose-leaf was removed from the path she had to tread, so clever that her father and uncle considered themselves fortunate to have secured him as a partner—and this man, this admirable compound of all manly virtues and all perfections, was *her* husband, her own for ever.

Providence had indeed been good to her, for her cup of happiness was full to overflowing. Her soft eyes would fill with tears as she looked at the stalwart form lying at her feet, and she would wonder how he could love such an insignificant little creature as herself, and what he could find in her to attract him ; for he was worthy of a Princess, and his sphere was a nobler and loftier one than she could ever reach. She wrote from Palermo to her father and to Mrs. Lascelles. Her letters were short, and those to Mr. Woodall only told that she was happy, and that

Ronald was very very good to her. To Mrs. Lascelles she was more effusive; some of the affection she bore to her husband found a vent in loving letters to his mother. She could not love him so deeply and so truly without also loving those who were dearest to him, and she had always been very fond of Mrs. Lascelles, whom she had learnt to look upon almost as a second mother even before she was engaged.

Now Mrs. Lascelles had really taken the place of a parent in Edith's heart, and as the image of her own dead mother grew fainter by the lapse of years, her mother-in-law took its place not unworthily. When the Consul's wife received the second letter from Sicily she wept, strong-minded woman as she was, and she thanked God for having given her wisdom and strength to guide her son aright. She had not dared to hope that the experiment would be so soon and so brilliantly successful. She had expected a few little difficulties, and thought that possibly it might take a

year or two before Ronald, with his eccentric ideas
and fantastic notions, would find out what a perfect
woman he had won, and how singularly fortunate he
was. But from Edith's letters, and also from Ronald's
own, she concluded that no passionate lovers could be
more devoted, no romantic couple happier. They
were wrapped up in each other, and in three short
weeks her son adored his wife more absolutely than
she could ever have hoped. She and Mr. Lascelles
read the letters over and over again together, and
rejoiced over the happiness of their children.

'You were right, dear,' said the Consul. 'You are
always right. How glad I am that we were firm with
Ronald.'

'You would have given way to the boy, if it had
not been for me,' said Mrs. Lascelles.

'I am afraid I should,' he replied. 'Thank God
that you came in on that evening.'

'Yes, indeed; you see I knew him better than he

knew himself. He positively worships Edith now. Did you ever read such an enthusiastic letter as hers ?'

'No,' answered the Consul; 'but his is not quite so warm.'

'You could not expect it,' said Mrs. Lascelles; 'men are always more reticent in writing. And besides, I think he is a little ashamed of his past folly.'

'Very likely.'

'And just see what he says,' continued she : '"Every day I discover some new virtue in my dear wife."'

'I hope he will go on discovering new perfections to the end of his days,' said Mr. Lascelles.

'No doubt he will. It was a difficult task to get over his exaggerated scruples; but now he is married and head over ears in love with her, there will not be a more devoted husband in all Europe.'

' He is the soul of honour, and such a good fellow !' exclaimed Mr. Lascelles. ' A son to be proud of, and he owes his happiness to his mother.'

' Not to me alone, dear,' answered Mrs. Lascelles, kissing her husband affectionately ; ' to his father as well, and, above all, to Providence. Let us be thankful, and hope that we shall find as good a husband as Ronald for dear little Teresina.'

' We do not want a better one,' said Mr. Lascelles.

' You could not find a better, if you looked all over the world,' replied his mother proudly.

CHAPTER XXIV.

THE STENTS SHOW THEIR CONFIDENCE.

Not many weeks later they settled in London, in a pretty little furnished house near Park Lane. Christmas was approaching. They were very busy at Woodalls' Bank, and the partners' private room was scarcely ever free from visitors for five minutes together. Although the deeds had not yet been signed, Ronald was already installed in this sanctum, to which he would have a legal right 'on and after' the first day of the new year.

The Stents had received Ronald and Edith very warmly, more warmly indeed than the former at all liked. For the number of dull dinners to which both were invited was enormous, and before he had gone through the clan he was wearied out, and declared that he would not accept any more invitations from any Stent whatever. It was sufficiently unfortunate that Clara had married one of the family and appeared by this act to have married the *whole* family. *He* had not done so, and he was not going to do so. They dined of course at his sister's; they went to Mr. Stent senior, to Mr. John and Mr. William. But when not only his brother-in-law's brothers, but also his brother-in-law's cousins, began to leave cards, he lost his temper. It was, perhaps, the first time that Edith had seen him really cross, except with stupid waiters, slow cabdrivers, or dilatory land-lords.

'You are not to return these visits, Edith,' he said.

'Why not, dear?' she inquired. 'They are, I believe, very respectable people.'

'Undoubtedly; but they are bores, and we know

bores enough already. We have not more than a hundred evenings a year, at most, on which we can dine out, and, if we do not take care, the Stents will monopolize ninety-nine of them.'

' But we can always refuse the invitations. And it is so rude not even to return a visit,' urged Edith, always unwilling to hurt anyone's feelings.

' You are too good for these folk,' exclaimed Ronald; ' you don't understand them. They presume on their connection having married my sister. They are not our style; they do not belong to the same world in any way. You will find it out by-and-by, when you come to know *my* friends.'

' They are certainly not so amusing as the people we met at Uncle Edward's,' admitted Edith.

' Of course not! they are pragmatical, narrow-minded, and out of society altogether. Now please do not think of being civil to them.'

' Very well, Ronald,' said Edith.

'Do not pay any visits except to the three houses where we have dined.'

'I am afraid Clara will be vexed,' observed Edith again.

'I do not care in the least. Now remember, I won't have it.'

And for the first time since their marriage, Ronald spoke imperiously to his wife, and left the room without a kind glance or a kiss. The fact was that Ronald was gradually forgetting the pretty loving ways he had acquired during the honeymoon. He was in a hurry to get away in the morning, and read the *Times* with his mouth full of toast and eggs, scarcely looking at Edith. He always kissed her before he started for the City, but the kiss was a very perfunctory one. He still returned by half-past five or six, and often took a cup of tea in the drawing room. This was the pleasantest part of the day to Edith. He would tell her anything new that had happened in the City, would ask her what she had been doing, would suggest the play or some other amusement for the evening, and would be thoroughly sociable for an hour. But even in this hour he was not loving. He never lay down at her feet now, nor looked into her eyes. He did not kiss her hand when she passed him cups of tea, as he used to do. He did not stroke her hair gently, nor admire her dress. He did not interrupt her when she told him little bits of feminine gossip, or of the shops where she had been, or the visits she had paid, but the old deference to every word of hers was gone. He did not seem to listen—certainly not to care. Sometimes he would take up the evening paper, or go down to his study to write letters. At dinner, in the presence of the servants, he was of course most kind and atten-tive—indeed he was always attentive—but she missed the frequent glances across to her, the smiles full of deep meaning (or none at all), the opportunities of rising and coming round to her chair, which he used formerly never to miss. The dinners were far better than those they had eaten in Sicily, but Edith preferred the Sicilian meals. Ronald evidently did not.

Very grievous to Edith was Ronald's omission of all the tender trifles which had made her honeymoon so happy. She argued indeed with herself that of course now he was busy, and had other and far weightier matters to attend to than saying pretty things to her, and petting her, and squeezing her hand, and kissing her on every occasion. She knew that he was keenly anxious to make himself indispensable at the Bank; that he devoted all the day to it, and often, when they were at home, spent hours in his study at work. But still she could not conquer a certain depression which crept over her when Ronald went off after a hurried kiss on her forehead, or when, on his arrival home, his first thought was to tell her that he had taken

stalls for the St. James's, or that they would go to a
concert at Willis's Rooms. He did not seem to care to
spend an evening quietly at home with her.

They had now been six weeks in London, and had
been alone together after dinner about six times.
Her company, she feared, was no longer amusing
enough for him. Surely on the rare occasions when
they neither went out nor had anybody with them,
he need not have rushed off to read 'Lubbock on
Banking,' or to study abstruse books on account-
keeping, directly after dinner! Her father was a
successful banker, but had never had occasion to
work like this. She was inclined to regret their
rough life in Sicily, and would willingly have exchanged all the theatres, concerts, and dinner-parties
for a few evenings such as she had spent at Palermo
and Messina.

The simple explanation was, of course, that a man can
play a part fairly successfully for a week or two, if he

has nothing else to think about, and no other object at the time except that part. When he returns to work and general society he falls back into his natural self. Ronald had never intended to act a part at all. He had honestly hoped that by studiously doing what other lovers did, by carefully and perseveringly pretending to be in love with his wife, by concentrating his thoughts on her virtues and beauties, he would succeed at last in being thoroughly and entirely in love with her. Perhaps the trial was too short. Possibly if the honeymoon had been extended to six months he might have succeeded. As it was, he certainly failed.

As soon as he reached London and returned to the Bank, the Bank absorbed his thoughts. He began to neglect the stage business which he had so carefully coached up. When he had done his work, when he returned home exhausted in mind and body, he required something more lively than merely his wife's conversation. That was pleasant enough in its way, but was insufficient to divert him and to prevent his dwelling on the business of the past day. He wanted bright scenes, exhilarating talk, nice people. The play served his turn ; and as he was enthusiastically fond of music, concerts were a delightful relaxation to him. It was not that he did not care for his wife. He loved her perhaps far better than in the first few days of their wedding-trip, when he studied every word before he spoke, every gesture, almost every kiss. He earnestly wished to please her and to make her happy, and he never gave way to regrets which would have been useless because too late, nor to dreams which would have been mischievous because impossible.

But just because he was active and busy, because his mind was full of other matters, and because he had no leisure for introspection, he soon not only neglected, but almost entirely forgot, the part he had determined to play. It happened sometimes that when he had finished his newspaper on the top of the omnibus which he generally took to the City, or when it rained and he had to hold up an umbrella, he would suddenly remember that he had only kissed his wife on the forehead before leaving, and had not said a single loving word to her on that morning. Then he would hope that she had not noticed it, and trust it would not grieve her, and before the omnibus reached St. Martin's-le-Grand he had forgotten all about it. Once, indeed, he returned from the corner of the street, and astonished Edith by coming into the dining-room and saying, 'I never kissed you this morning.' But he did not generally remember his omission till it was too late to repair it.

One dull afternoon, when the gas burnt dimly and seemed to make the gloom of the City darker than ever, two cards were brought into Mr. Woodall's private room at the Bank.

He passed them over to Ronald. 'They are for

you, I think. See them in the waiting-room while I shorthand this letter to the Banbury Cake Company. I do not like their way of doing business, and I shall tell them so.'

The cards bore the names 'Mr. Stent' and 'Mr. George Stent.' Ronald went out into the waiting-room to them.

'How do you do?' said George Stent, holding out his hand and smiling.

'Good afternoon, Mr. Lascelles,' said Mr. Stent, senior.

'What can I do for you?' asked Ronald, after having shaken hands with his friends. He was quaking inwardly, though he did not show his nervousness. Courage is by some authors defined to be the art of concealing fear. If the definition is correct, Ronald was very brave indeed. It was an unheard-of circumstance for the chief of the Stent clan to leave his offices during business hours, except on business connected with Stent and Cowcroft. He had never come to the Bank before. Now he came with his eldest son, obviously there was something in the wind, and Ronald connected that something with the directions he had recently given Edith. Probably the two had come to expostulate with him. He must be firm. He would be courteous if he could, but he would not give way. He would absolutely and finally decline to be swallowed up by the Stent maelstrom. If the nephews and cousins thought that the imposing nature of the deputation could make him give way, they should find out their mistake. All this passed through his mind in a few seconds, while he waited for his brother-in-law to speak.

'We should like to see Mr. Woodall,' said George.

'Oh! I beg your pardon,' exclaimed Ronald, quite relieved. 'On business?'

'Yes, on business,' answered Mr. Stent senior.

'On important and not unpleasing business,' added George sententiously.

'Kindly wait half a minute,' said Ronald. 'My uncle is just short-handing an important letter; but I will tell him you are here, and I am sure he will not keep you an instant longer than he can help.'

'They will be surprised,' said Mr. Stent, when Ronald had closed the door.

'But it is undoubtedly the proper thing to do,' remarked George.

'I think so. It will be taken as a distinct sign that we all approve of the connection, and wish to support it and strengthen it.'

'We do not owe anything to the Arbuthnots,' said George.

'On the contrary. They have been shabby more than once, and they too frequently make mistakes. Young Arbuthnot is very careless.'

'Quite so. But they will regret the step we are taking.'

' It is only right that when an old-established Bank deserts its wholesome traditions, and the junior partner leads a fast and disreputable life, City firms of standing should show their disapproval by with-drawing their accounts.'

' It is quite right, as we all decided last night,' said George.

' I understand that Ronald will be a partner as from the first of January,' remarked Mr. Stent.

' Tuesday week,' observed George. 'A very good thing indeed. He is very steady, I hear from all sides, and works like a Trojan.'

' A most estimable young man,' said Mr. Stent.

' Quite so,' remarked George. ' An ornament to the family.'

' I suppose it will last ?' hinted his father.

' Undoubtedly. Ronald is no fool. He has gained

a position very quickly and very cleverly, and I have no doubt he will keep it.'

'He has good friends, too,' said Mr. Stent. 'Mr. Woodall will appreciate him all the more in consequence of our coming. I should think they would give you their Stock Exchange business now.'

'I hope so. In any case Ronald is likely to do them a lot of good, partly through us and partly through his West End acquaintances. I saw him yesterday afternoon with Lord Caerlyon.'

'Did you really, George?' asked Mr. Stent almost incredulously. 'Where?'

'On the steps of the Palmflower Club. They were talking quite intimately.'

'Lord Caerlyon is very rich, but extravagant and fond of racing,' observed Mr. Stent.

'The aristocracy,' said George, 'is entitled to do many things which we, as business men, have no right to meddle with. It would be suicide if you or

I were to own a race horse, or be seen in the betting-ring. But Lord Caerlyon is in a very different position. You know, father,' he added, lowering his voice, 'we must move a little with the times. We cannot quite afford to condemn all amusements, and we rather like a little fun ourselves now and then.'

'If it is thoroughly moral and Christian,' observed Mr. Stent.

'Of course. But we must not condemn too harshly those who do not see the sin of certain pursuits we object to. Great noblemen and financiers have always been allowed a certain latitude. But what a time old Woodall is keeping us!'

At that moment they were summoned.

'You are no doubt surprised to see us, Mr. Woodall,' said George, after they had all sat down.

'Well, I did not expect the pleasure. In what way can I serve you?' asked the banker.

'Mr. Woodall,' began Mr Stent, senior, 'you are no doubt very busy, and I won't waste your time by beating about the bush.'

'Thank you. I *am* rather busy just now. It is the close of the year, and this nephew of mine is going to strengthen the Bank by becoming a partner on the first of January, which makes a good many changes necessary.'

'Precisely. That is what brings us here. Mr. Ronald Lascelles is, I am proud to say, a connection of ours. My son has married his sister.'

Mr. Woodall bowed. Ronald almost wished she had not.

'Now, sir,' continued the old man pompously, 'you are aware that the members of my family are all in business!'

Mr. Woodall bowed again.

'They are all, I may say, in a good steady way of business. No wild speculations for me, sir, nor for them. They will never make a million, but they keep on scraping it up, sir, scraping it up bit by bit.'

'No doubt, no doubt,' assented the banker, wondering what he was driving at.

'You may be aware, sir, that there are three firms in which the family are represented. There is my own, Stent and Cowcroft, of which I need say nothing, as it is so well known.'

'Quite right,' said Mr. Woodall, 'we all know Stent and Cowcroft's.'

'Precisely. Then there is Stent Brothers, the stock-brokers, the partners in which are my son George here and his youngest brother William.'

'Stent Brothers,' began George, 'are doing a fair steady business. We don't compete with the brokers who encourage gambling, so we do not turn over any-thing like what we might.'

Mr. Woodall bowed again ; but being anxious to hear

what the Stents wanted, he said nothing. Did they wish to negotiate a loan?

'Lastly,' resumed Mr. Stent, 'there is Stent and Son in Leadenhall Avenue, in which my brother and his son, Mr. William A. Stent, are the only partners. Their business, sir, is principally tea, and they own a few trading-vessels.'

'Indeed!' observed Mr. Woodall, as Mr. Stent was evidently waiting for him to speak.

'Now, sir, all these firms wish to open an account with you.'

'With us?' asked Mr. Woodall, surprised. 'Why leave your present bankers?'

'That, sir,' replied Mr. Stent, 'is a question I would prefer not to answer. I do not wish to injure Arbuthnot's in any way. But we decline to bank with them any longer, and we desire to show our confidence in yourself, and in Mr. Ronald Lascelles, by transferring our credits to your Bank.'

'I feel very much honoured,' said Mr. Woodall, 'and I am very glad that Ronald has been the means of securing to us such excellent customers.'

'We were sure you would be pleased,' said Mr. Stent, 'and we were anxious to do Mr. Lascelles a good turn. I wish to add that the three firms I have mentioned all keep an account at the Bank of England: this they propose to continue.'

'Of course,' said Mr. Woodall.

'The money they have at the Bank of England is a sort of nest-egg,' observed Mr. Stent. 'The balances do not move much. It is not often operated on. We should bring you all our bills without exception.'

'We shall be happy to discount good paper,' said Mr. Woodall, cautiously.

'Sir,' replied Mr. Stent, 'Stent and Cowcroft and Stent and Son take nothing but first-class names. Stent Brothers require no accommodation of this sort, do you, George?'

'No,' answered he; 'we only want moderate advances on stocks and shares.'

The details of the arrangement were then discussed. Ronald was genuinely surprised. The accounts offered to his Bank were by no means unimportant, and he felt that to have obtained the voluntary support of the Stents was a feather in his cap. He thought of the proverb that nothing succeeds like success. Would any member of the Stent family have lent him ten pounds if he had not married Edith? Probably not.

It was arranged that the partners in the various firms should call on the following day to sign their names and complete the necessary formalities. Mr. Stent senior and George then bowed themselves out with many civil protestations. When they had gone Mr. Woodall looked sharply at Ronald.

'Did you ask them to bring their accounts here?' he asked.

'Certainly not, sir. I never even hinted it. I do not allude to the Bank's business to anyone, let alone the Stents.'

'You are not very fond of them?' asked Mr. Woodall again.

'Not very, sir. They are very respectable, and all that, but very dull, you know.'

Mr. Woodall smiled. 'You are quite sure that you have dropped no suggestion to any one that we should like them as customers?—some one who may have gone and told them, you know?'

'Quite sure, sir. The only person outside to whom I have ever spoken about our affairs at all, is my wife.'

'Quite right, Ronald. Never open your mouth to any one else about what goes on here. Edith is a clever woman, and may be trusted. But take my advice, and do not say anything to her if by chance there should be a hitch some day—awkward times to get over, or a panic in the City. Such things may happen, you know.'

' Yes, sir,' answered Ronald.

' Well, at such times don't tell your wife. Women are too nervous and too excitable to be trusted. They may have hysterics, or be frightened out of their wits, or something of the sort, and then the doctor is sent for, and some fellow hears about it and says the Bank is going. Whatever happens, keep your own counsel.'

' I will, sir.'

' That is all right, and I trust, indeed, that no such crisis will occur. When it does, and if it does, keep cool and think things over carefully. Don't get flustered. Now about these Stents. Of course Stent and Cowcrofts are solid—very solid ?'

' No doubt.'

' But,' continued Mr. Woodall, ' my experience tells me never to believe in the strength of firms in which partners are fools. Old Stent is a pompous fellow, but he is not stupid. But I believe that most of his sons are mere pedantic asses.'

'So do I,' assented Ronald, very warmly.

'That being the case, I don't trust their judgment. Just keep your weather eye open, Ronald. If I am out of the way, be very careful about giving Stent Brothers and Stent and Son accommodation. Don't breathe a word, and, whatever happens, don't offend them if you can help it. But just be careful.'

CHAPTER XXV.

RICHMOND.

WHEN the winter drew towards its end, and Ronald had for some time been a full-blown partner in Woodall's, the pressure of his work diminished. He had mastered the routine of the business, and made the acquaintance of the majority of the Bank's customers and agents, had taken a run to Lancashire to visit some of the mills with whom his uncle had frequent transactions, and was now thoroughly initiated in the mysteries of book-keeping. So he found himself comparatively at leisure, and was often able to leave the City soon after four o'clock, without neglecting his duties in the least. But he no

longer went straight home. In the early days of
their stay in London, he made the best of his way
to Park Lane as soon as he could lock up his safe.
Lately, however, he had begun to look in occasionally
at the Palmflower Club in St. James's Street, just to
hear what they said in the West End. Soon the look-
in extended to an hour or so, and after a time he
stopped there daily before going home. He met many
of his old friends at the Palmflower. St. Clair was a
member; St. Clair had married his old love, and
the two enjoyed themselves immensely. Ronald
went home with his friend one afternoon, and the next
day Mrs. St. Clair called on Edith. Insignificant little
woman as she was, she possessed all the liveliness and
knowledge of the world which Edith lacked altogether.
They dined at the St. Clair's in their tiny house in
Brompton, and Ronald was delighted with the dinner,
with the way everything was done, and with the people
they met. The talk was lively and continuous. The

last play, the last fashionable scandal, and the prospects for the season were all discussed in turn in a tone which Edith failed to understand. She did not take to Mrs. St. Clair at all. On their way home she confided to Ronald in a horror-stricken voice that his friend's wife painted her face. She was appalled when Ronald merely said :

'Very likely. Lots of women do. She has not got such a good complexion as you, dear.'

'I don't trust any woman that paints!' exclaimed Edith.

'You need not. You are not called upon to trust everybody you meet, though, by-the-bye, Mrs. St. Clair's crime is a very venial one.'

'But surely I cannot be friends with people I am unable to trust?' asked Edith.

'Why not? If they give nice dinners, and make themselves agreeable, and talk well, what more do you want?'

'I should feel such a hypocrite, being civil to a person I disliked,' said Edith.

'Nonsense, dear. You are too enthusiastic. There is surely a medium course. There is no occasion to tell Mrs. St. Clair, or people like her, all your secrets, nor to make a bosom-friend of her. But you can be friendly all the same, and find her very good company.'

'I do not think she is good company,' said Edith. 'She is dreadfully frivolous.'

'My dear child,' replied Ronald, 'you must really get rid of some of your provincial notions. Who makes your dresses, by-the-bye?'

Now up to this period Ronald had always thought that Edith dressed to perfection, and no doubt her travelling dresses and morning gowns were fairly well made, and admirably set off by her graceful figure. But at the St. Clairs' she had somehow looked dowdy. The material of her dress was very good, but the colour did not suit her; and as to the cut, it was entirely wanting in style. Ugly and small as was Mrs. St. Clair, she positively looked better than Edith. This must be attended to at once. Edith scarcely knew whether to be pleased or sorry at the interest Ronald now took in her toilette. It was a form of interest she scarcely understood. He came back early from the City next day, and spent an hour with her at Madame Christine's, the most fashionable dressmaker in London; and then he went the round of sundry milliners with her, and made her try on a dozen bonnets. But when a few days later she consulted him about altering a certain morning dress, and asked his opinion about a bonnet she was making at home, to save the absurd prices charged at the shop, she was astonished to hear him say :

'Oh, don't ask me, and do not go patching up old things. Let Madame Christine make you a new dress when you want one.'

'But, Ronald, I do not want a new dress for *every* dinner-party.'

'I do not care. You are to look nice, and I wish my wife to be one of the best dressed women in London. No home-made rubbish, please.'

'But think of the expense, Ronald dear,' she ventured to expostulate. 'That dress you ordered the other day will cost over twenty pounds.'

'You have lots of money,' was his reply. 'What is your four hundred a year for? and if it is not enough, come to me for more.'

And, as a matter of fact, they had plenty of money; quite as much as they wanted. At Christmas, Ronald had received from the bank what the two Woodalls considered a fair remuneration for his eight months' incessant work: twelve hundred pounds. The articles of partnership provided that he should draw quarterly at the same rate, in anticipation of profits. And Ronald knew perfectly well that these sums were far within the boundary of prudence. The profits made were very large—far larger than Mr. Stent senior had estimated when he had discussed the matter with his sons. So he was determined that his wife should not have the excuse of economy to dress badly. The money would never have been his if it had not been for Edith, and as much of it as she could possibly require should be spent on her. She should have a phaeton and a pair of ponies when the fine weather began, even though they might have to dispose of it for nothing when they went to Portino next year.

May brought an increase of work to Ronald, and an increased number of invitations to him and his wife. Mr. Edward Woodall had several threatenings of gout, and was more than once prevented from appearing in the City. Increased responsibility was thrown on the junior partner at a particularly trying time. For it was a period of speculative enterprise, of high prices, and immense activity. Small people were making thousands in a few days. New companies were brought out daily, and their shares made large premiums. Old-fashioned men who stuck to their old ways were laughed at and left behind. Some of the best and most respectable firms supported new undertakings which their fathers and grandfathers would have called swindles. It was difficult for a young man not to be carried away by the general enthusiasm and belief in a golden future, but Ronald mistrusted his own judgment, and would do nothing important without consulting Mr. Woodall. When the latter was kept at Wimbledon by the gout, the junior would often run down to Heath Lodge by an afternoon train, and spend the evening with the invalid to ascertain his views on the new schemes proposed to the Bank, the new customers introduced, and the position of old ones who had embarked in new ventures. For Ronald had from the beginning made up his mind that he was only a trustee for his wife. It was her money

with which he had to deal, and it was only in his
capacity as her husband that he was a partner in the
bank. If he had bought a share in it with his own
funds he would probably have been bolder. But, as
he had decided on that remarkable evening at Portino,
the Woodalls should never repent having taken him
as a partner. It should never be said that they had
made a bad bargain, and that the bank had lost
money by their confidence in him. He was therefore
so cautious that even Mr. Woodall occasionally chaffed
him about it, and said that he had never seen so old
a head on such young shoulders.

Ronald was unceasing in his efforts to find out all
the ins and outs of the various matters proposed to
him, and even with the best names as a guarantee he
took very little on trust. The information he thus
collected and was able to lay before Mr. Woodall was
invaluable. Ronald spent several nights travelling to
investigate, as well as he could by a flying visit,

manufactories, shipbuilding yards and engineering establishments on which money was required, or which had been turned into limited companies. Often he was unable to go himself. Then he sent persons whom he could trust, with a list of questions to which they had to ascertain the answers. But if their report was encouraging, and the business appeared promising, he seldom undertook it without a personal investigation, and it was strange how often such an investigation showed that his agents had been deceived. Many people in the City began to smile when Woodalls' bank was mentioned, and said that such old-fashioned over-cautious folks would never get on. But Ronald was not to be diverted from his path, and was at work morning, noon, and night.

Edith was, of course, very much alone during this period. She knew enough of Ronald's absorbing occupations to forgive his absence from home, but she thought he worked far too hard and was unnecessarily

anxious. She ventured to argue with him once or
twice, but he replied that he had been entrusted with
her money and her father's, and that he must look
after it. Over and over again was Ronald obliged to
send a message at the eleventh hour to decline a
dinner-party, or to tell her to go to the play with
Clara, as he could not escort her. Clara was fortunately well, and able to go about, so she helped her
sister-in-law over her loneliness. At the beginning of
June the pressure diminished a little in intensity as
Mr. Woodall was able to attend regularly. One day,
George Stent, who, being now a regular customer, was
frequently at the bank, sent in for Ronald. He came
out of his room looking very tired and fagged.

'Ronald,' said he good - naturedly, 'you look
thoroughly done up. You have really been working
too hard.'

'We have been very busy,' said Ronald, smiling
faintly.

'Yes; these are busy times, and you have had all the work on your own shoulders. Edith and Clara are both getting quite anxious about you.'

'There is no occasion for any anxiety.'

'At any rate, you may as well come out of the City when you have a chance, and take a little relaxation. Cassoni and his wife are coming down to Richmond with us by-and-by, and we are going to dine at the Star and Garter. Go and fetch Edith and come too. It will do you much good, and revive your spirits.'

Cassoni was a young Italian artist who had settled in London, and whom Mr. Stent senior had taken up. It has already been mentioned that Mr. Stent bought pictures, and Cassoni had been pointed out to him as a rising young man whose works were sure to increase in value. So Mr. Stent purchased the best of those he had shown in the winter at the Belgian Gallery, and had given him an order for another. He was a pleasant, attractive young fellow, and had married a charming, simple English girl, whom he had fallen in with at a country house where he was painting the owner's portrait. Mr. Stent senior having patronized him, he had been adopted by the clan, and Ronald was delighted that a little variety was thus introduced into their dinner-parties. George's offer was tempting. The City was insufferably stuffy. The sky looked yellow, but Ronald knew that a few miles further west it was blue and bright. Next to the sparkling waters of the sea, and the white sails of the *Santa Lucia*, he yearned for the silvery reaches of the Thames, and for a breath of healthy fresh air.

'When do you start?' he asked doubtfully.

'At half-past two—directly after lunch. We want to have a couple of hours on the river before dinner. Come, send Edith a telegraph message, and then go home and fetch her.'

'I should like to come, very much,' said Ronald, still hesitatingly.

'Well, why not, then? Have you anything very particular to do to-day?'

'No; nothing beyond the ordinary business. But one never knows what may turn up.'

'You need not stop for what may or may not happen,' said George. 'You know I am a thorough man of business myself. I never take a whole day. But in the summer, if I can get through my work in the morning, I do not see why I should not occasionally have a run into the country for a change.'

'I will see if Mr. Woodall can spare me,' said Ronald.

'Queer chap!' thought George. 'A year ago that fellow was never to be found at his office except when he could not help it. He was always about somewhere, playing croquet, or flirting, or dancing, or something worse. And now he's as steady as an old Bank of England clerk, and never thinks of anything but business.'

Mr. Woodall at once told Ronald to go.

'You have been too hard at it,' he said, 'and an afternoon will do you good. You want a longer holiday than that, and I hope you will soon get it. Now make yourself scarce ; I know what there is to attend to, so don't worry.'

Ronald promised to meet his brother-in-law at the Star and Garter. He would drive down with Edith in their victoria, as George's carriage could not possibly hold more than four. Then they would order dinner, and all spend the afternoon on the river. Edith was delighted, and soon they were rolling smoothly along the Knightsbridge Road. With no thought of impending evil, they both chatted more gaily than they had done for some time. Ronald strove to get rid of the City cobwebs and succeeded. He had taken flannels with him, and when they met their friends, proposed to dispense with a waterman, and paddle them about in a tub. It was a stiff task he set himself, for six people make a heavy cargo for one man, particularly when he is out of training. However, they were in no hurry. He sculled up gently with the tide towards Twickenham, and by-and-by Cassoni threw off his coat, and said he must help. Clara was in good spirits. George Stent had got rid of much of his stiffness, but did not talk, which was a relief, while Mrs. Cassoni and Edith enjoyed themselves thoroughly. It was nearly seven o'clock when they returned to the hotel. At once Ronald retired to change his dress, promising to join the others on the lawn, where they would walk till the dinner was ready. When he descended the steps to look for them, he heard a voice which sent the blood rushing to his face. It was long since he had heard it, but yet it seemed but yesterday. It proceeded from a group standing on the gravel walk just under the coffee-room. There were two handsomely dressed ladies surrounded by several men. One of the ladies, she whose voice he had recognised, was tall, and had a beautiful figure, which was shown off to perfection by a close-fitting foulard dress. She wore a Gainsborough hat, which shaded a dark but fascinating face. Dark black eyes, a short nose, rather inclined to be *retroussé*, and a small mouth with full red lips, made up a very attractive total, which seemed to demand admiration, and to challenge a comparison with more classical beauties. The black eyes were looking mischievously at one of the men, whose back was turned to Ronald. Suddenly they glanced over the man's shoulder and met Ronald's gaze. He raised his hat, while she stepped forward with outstretched hands.

'Mr. Lascelles!' she exclaimed.

'Miss Monsell!' said he.

'No,' she answered; 'I am Lady Redbourne now. Did you not know that I was married?'

'Yes, I heard,' he answered; 'but I forgot at the moment. Allow me to congratulate you.'

She shrugged her shoulders.

'I don't know that there is anything to be congratulated about.'

'Is his lordship here?' asked Ronald. 'You must honour me by introducing me to him.'

'Here?' she said. 'Certainly not. I don't suppose he is up yet. He does not generally get up till dark. He is a dreadful invalid, you know.'

'And you are his nurse?' asked Ronald, suddenly remembering that the American heiress had married a noble lord old enough to be her grandfather.

'Is it likely? No, I enjoy myself, as I have a right to do. Now let me introduce you. Captain Verney, Mr. Lascelles, an old friend of mine. Lord Castleton, Mrs. Hardy, Mr. Lascelles. Mr. Munden—oh! I see you know each other,' said Lady Redbourne, as Ronald shook hands with the last mentioned.

'Yes,' said Mr. Munden. 'Mr. Lascelles and I have often met at the club. But I have not

seen you much lately,' he added, turning politely to
Ronald.

'No, I have been too busy. I am in the City now,'
replied Ronald.

'In the City? Indeed! I was not aware that you
had left Somerset House. I ought to have heard, as
I'm in the City myself,' said Mr. Munden, who was a
perfect man about town, faultless in his get-up, calm
in his manner, ready with the usual smart talk and
full of the latest gossip.

'I have been in the City nearly six months,' said
Ronald.

'Indeed! May I ask where?' inquired Mr. Munden.

'Woodalls' bank.'

'Oh! of course. I ought to have known. But I
had no idea *you* were the new partner. Allow me to
congratulate you.'

'Come, Mr. Lascelles, let us take a turn,' said her
ladyship, placing her hand on Ronald's arm and in-

terrupting the conversation. 'We have a lot to talk about.'

Ronald complied. He had seen that face not so very long ago—much more recently than Lady Redbourne thought. It was on the way from Paris to Marseilles.

'Now tell me all about yourself,' said she, when they had moved out of ear-shot. 'What have you been doing since I behaved so shamefully to you at Ascot, two years ago? Oh, what a long time!'

She looked into his face as she spoke, her dark eyes softening. They were velvety and gentle now, and the mischief had died away out of them.

'You use harsh words about yourself, Lady Redbourne.'

'No harsher than I deserve,' she replied, quickly. 'But it was mamma who did it, you know. It was not really my fault. I cried my eyes out because she would not let me speak to you.'

'They have entirely recovered, then,' said Ronald flippantly; 'for they are brighter than ever.'

'You talk nonsense, as you always did, Ronald,' said she calmly, addressing him by his christian name. ' But you talk very pleasant nonsense sometimes. Do you recollect that afternoon at Lord's, at the Oxford and Cambridge match ?'

She pressed his arm gently.

' As if I could ever forget !' said Ronald. ' It was one of the happiest days of my life. I trusted you then, and believed in you. I thought you the most lovely woman I had ever seen, and the most attractive.'

' And now ?' asked Lady Redbourne. 'Have I turned ugly already?' She stopped, and looked at him inquiringly.

' No. You know very well that you are more beautiful than ever,' said Ronald.

At that moment they met a party walking along the

lawn in the opposite direction. Ronald nodded to them.

'Who are those people?' asked Lady Redbourne. 'Badly dressed women, anyhow.'

Ronald flushed scarlet, and dropped his companion's arm.

'One of the badly dressed women is my wife, Lady Redbourne. I ought to have told you that I also am married.'

'Oh! I'm so sorry. I really did not mean it, Ronald,' exclaimed she, impetuously. 'Do forgive me! It was just like my stupid bluntness. Which was your wife?'

'It is of no consequence, Lady Redbourne. There is nothing to forgive. I must join them, as they are expecting me to dinner. Good-bye.'

'Stay, Ronald! I cannot let you go like this. Remember, I have not seen you for two years. You would surely not leave me in anger?' She leant on his arm, and looked beseechingly into his face.

They again passed, George Stent, with Mrs. Cassoni on one side and Edith on the other. George stared, while Edith looked uncomfortable.

'That is my wife,' said Ronald; 'the fair one.'

'She would be charming,' observed Lady Redbourne, turning to watch the retreating group, 'if she were better dressed. Now, Ronald, you must not be angry with me,' she went on, volubly. 'I consider myself entitled to speak with authority. Do I dress well? Just look at me.'

'Of course you do!' answered Ronald, as he looked at that exquisitely fitting, light-maize foulard, the coquettish hat, and admirable gloves, which were a poem in themselves. And he was not able to confine his attention entirely to the elegant costume; the wearer obtained the larger share of his undisguised admiration.

'I am glad you acknowledge it,' said she, with a toss of her pretty head. 'They call me the best-dressed woman about; so I think I have a right to talk.'

'Certainly,' said Ronald; 'no one has a better right. You preach by example, which is more than most people do. But not everyone can dress like you do, Lady Redbourne. It is an ideal very few can attain.'

'I am quite sure that your wife could do far better than she does. I shall be very glad to help. I will give you the address of the people she must go to.'

'I have sent her to Madame Christine's,' Ronald ventured to observe.

'Madame Christine? She is no good at all. Christine does well enough for very many people, who can tell her exactly what to do; but she has no style of her own—no *chic* at all. Worth is the only man. He comes to town several times in the season, and, besides, it is so easy to go to Paris. I will give you a letter to

Worth. He will take care of any of *my* friends, and you will hardly know your wife when he has dressed her. She is not at all an ugly little woman.'

Ronald could not be angry. If a man had spoken in this manner, he would have knocked him down; Lady Redbourne was a woman, and was too deliciously pretty. She said the rudest things in a simple, impulsive way, which seemed to take all the sting out of them. And she, undoubtedly, dressed very well— so well, that he could not but confess that the ladies of his party looked frumps in comparison. He would certainly go and see this great Mr. Worth. But now he must return to his people.

'I really must be off now, Lady Redbourne. I see my folks have already gone in; we are dining in number seven.'

'Don't go, Ronald,' said she. 'We are in number six. Come and dine with us.' She looked into his eyes imploringly. They were again soft, velvety, and beseeching. They were the eyes of the dreams and visions he had tried so hard to forget; yet he strove to resist them, and refused. Again she coaxed and caressed him, and at last summoned the rest of her party to her aid.

'Captain Verney,' she cried, 'and Mrs. Hardy, help me to persuade Mr. Lascelles to dine with us. He insists on going back to his wife.'

'Is Mrs. Lascelles alone here?' asked Mrs. Hardy.

'Oh no,' exclaimed Lady Redbourne; 'there is a whole party with her.'

'Then surely,' said Mrs. Hardy, raising another fine pair of eyes, grey this time, on poor Ronald, 'you could not refuse Lady Redbourne's request.'

'Really . . .' stammered Ronald.

'And I have not seen him for two years,' exclaimed the impulsive woman. 'We have not had a chance of saying a word yet.'

' You could send a note to your friends,' suggested Captain Verney.

' Of course he can,' cried Lady Redbourne. ' No, I shan't let you run away and tell them, or you will not come back. Now do not go on like a girl who is asked to sing. Write a line on a card. Here is my pocket-book.'

She produced a tiny thing of morocco leather and gold, and pulled a little pencil out of it. After another struggle, Ronald yielded. He wrote on the back of a card :

' Have met Munden and Lady Redbourne, who insist on my dining with them. Please excuse me.' He placed the name of the insignificant Munden first. But probably that gentleman's invitation would not have tempted him away. The card was dispatched by a waiter, and they adjourned to dinner. Lady Redbourne made Ronald sit by her, and devoted herself very specially to him. The party was a merry one. Captain Verney told of some funny adventures in India. Mrs. Hardy was full of fun and repartee. Lord Castleton, whose dinner it turned out to be, was a charming host, and very good naturedly allowed Ronald to monopolise Lady Redbourne. But the conversation was too general to give his lordship any cause for jealousy. Somehow, Ronald felt at home with these people, far more so than he did with the Stents, or at Portino, or even at his own house. The dinner was excellent and well served, and, though he was occasionally troubled with pangs of remorse, they were stifled by Lady Redbourne's soft glances and softer words. When the dessert was on the table Lady Redbourne rose.

'Will you get me my cloak, Captain Verney?' she said. 'I should like to take a turn in the garden. The evening is so exquisite. Ronald, will you give me your arm? You may smoke, if you like.'

Ronald was obliged to comply. Perhaps he did so not unwillingly. Silently they walked across the now-deserted lawn. Lady Redbourne was carrying her hat, which she swung abstractedly by its ribbon. They reached the terrace and looked out on the Thames. The moon had risen, and cast a silver band across the the smooth water. The dark trees were whispering very softly in the gentle summer wind.

'Do you remember such another night, Ronald, when we sat on the balcony at Lady Golderby's?'

'Aye, indeed,' he answered, 'you danced with me many times on that evening, and you gave me a flower which I kept for ever so long.'

'I was happy then,' she said, raising her arm to her brow, 'because I thought you loved me, Ronald. But I am wretched now, though I have all I can wish for! Are *you* happy?' She gazed into his eyes inquiringly. The moon cast a pale light over his face as he shook his head doubtfully.

'I do not know,' he answered. 'Certainly I ought to be very happy.'

'I made a great mistake,' she went on in a low voice, her face close to Ronald's. 'My poor mother thought she was acting for the best, but she was wrong. After all, being "her ladyship" does not amount to much. I wish I were plain Alma Monsell again! —No!' she added after a pause, 'I forgot: I do not wish it. But I am glad to have seen you again, Ronald. We were very fond of each other, dear.'

With a sad bewitching smile, she made him answer, almost against his will,

'And you are sweeter and more fascinating than ever,' he whispered. 'Oh! Alma, how could you be so cruel? Too late! too late!'

'Perhaps we should not have got on together,' said Lady Redbourne, placing her hand gently on Ronald's shoulder. 'Perhaps it is better as it is.

But my heart is very sore, Ronald, very sore indeed. Can you ever forgive me for having jilted you ? Look into my face, and say you forgive me from your heart.'

Now the moon shone with its wan light on her upturned face. Her black eyes were darker and deeper than ever, while her thin nostrils quivered as her breath came more quickly, and her lovely full lips were parted as she looked anxiously for her answer. It came. An arm stole round her waist and two warm lips were pressed against hers.

'They will be looking for us,' she whispered after a few minutes. 'There is a man in the corner watching us now. We must move away, for everybody can see us by this moonlight. I will take you home in my brougham. I cannot let you go—I can't indeed. You must not refuse me, darling. Perhaps it is the last time we shall ever meet.'

Ronald scarcely knew what he was doing. Lady

Redbourne put on her hat and swept through the hall. The brougham was at the door.

'Tell Lord Castleton that I have gone home,' she said to the porter.

And they drove off.

CHAPTER XXVI.

SUSPENSE.

In No. 7, at the Star and Garter, the dinner was very quiet. A great depression had fallen on the party. Even merry Signor Cassoni could not be jovial when he looked at Edith's sad face, for she had not yet learnt to conceal her feelings. She felt utterly wretched, and she showed it. Probably if she had not seen Ronald walk up and down with that pretty person she might have been less unhappy. But she had seen too much to be able to enjoy the dinner.

The sky was still blue; the trees were clad in fresh young leaves. The Thames shone in gold and purple under the setting sun, and the green lawn was still

dotted with smartly dressed people. But for Edith
the heavens were overcast and she saw not the fresh
green, nor heeded the smart people. Ronald had left
her unkindly, rudely, to go off with some old flame of
his. It might be nothing serious—it was probably mere
thoughtlessness—but it was dreadful all the same.
She tried to laugh, but her laugh sounded hollow;
she endeavoured to talk, but her voice stuck in her
throat. Oh! if she could only have been alone, and
have allowed her tears full vent. With Cassoni
looking at her, his large eyes full of pity, with Clara
squeezing her hand and whispering, 'Never mind, dear,
keep up your spirits,' and George Stent pursing up
his mouth and putting on his sternest expression, she
felt as if the dinner would never end. Ronald would
surely come in as soon as it was over, and then all
would be right again. Worse almost than his defection
was the construction that George would put on it.
She could read his face, and, knowing that there was

no love lost between him and her husband, she dreaded the result of Ronald's indiscretion. She did not know what would happen, and therefore trembled all the more. She shivered when she thought of the mysterious mischief George Stent might do him. She had long ago guessed that the Stents were not really well-disposed, though outwardly so friendly, and she had no means of gauging their power for evil ; therefore, she thought that it was immense. The tact of the little Italian and the quiet good sense of his wife helped her through the endless repast. When it was over George Stent asked her whether she would like to take a turn on the terrace. She looked appealingly at Clara, but when her husband suggested anything Clara always approved. 'I would rather rest a little,' she summoned courage to falter.

'Let us go out,' suggested Cassoni, 'and let Mrs. Lascelles have a little quiet.'

George rang for the bill, and made a resolute

attempt to remain behind the others, wishing to have what he called a little quiet talk with his sister-in-law. But in this endeavour he was defeated by Cassoni, who would not go till he could take George with him. Edith was at last left alone, and she listened impatiently for Ronald's step. If she could only see him before he met the others, she might conjure the danger. For she knew well that her husband would not brook the slightest remark from any of the Stents, however much his conduct might justify it. But no Ronald came. Tears slowly forced their way to her eyes. She wept bitterly but silently, for as time went on she felt that there might be worse things than the vengeance of an outraged Stent. Nine o'clock had long struck, and the guests were gradually departing. At last some one entered the room. She raised her head, hoping against hope for Ronald. It was George Stent.

'It is of no use waiting,' he said; 'your precious

husband has driven off alone with that person, Lady Redbourne, it seems.'

'It is not true,' she cried indignantly. 'How can you say such things?'

'I am not in the habit of making statements I cannot substantiate,' answered he, in his usual sententious style. 'I saw him kissing her on the terrace, and have since ascertained that they went off together in her ladyship's brougham.'

Of course, George Stent was very angry, but there mingled with his anger a little satisfaction at his forecast of Ronald's future having come true after all. Any man of ordinary feeling would have been silent about what he had seen on the terrace—would, at any rate, not have told the wrong-doer's wife. But George was not a man of ordinary feeling. His motives of propriety were very rigid, while he did not even know of the existence of such a quality as tact. The former had been grossly outraged; the latter being unknown to him, he could not observe. He thrust the dagger into Edith's heart without any special malice, merely because he disliked Ronald, and this was a chance of giving his feelings vent. If he had been asked why he told Edith what he knew must hurt her deeply, he would have replied calmly that it was his duty to put the poor wife on her guard against such a man. Nobody could have persuaded him that he was committing a mean, ungentlemanly act. He would not have resented such an accusation. He would simply have stared at his accuser, and thought he was off his head. There are certain people whose hide is like that of a rhinoceros.

' We will go home, then,' said Edith coldly, after a pause. ' Where are the others ? Please fetch them.'

They soon came, George having been careful to tell them what he had seen and heard. Cassoni was quite disgusted at being made the recipient of what ought to have remained a dead secret, and exclaimed,

'You surely did not tell her?' while Clara only gasped.

'Will you come with us, Edith?' asked George, when the carriage was ready. 'Mr. and Mrs. Cassoni can drive home in your victoria.'

'No, thank you,' answered she, shrinking back.

'But you cannot drive home alone!' exclaimed he. 'All that way at this time of night.'

'Why not?' asked Edith coldly; 'it is my own carriage. I prefer being alone, thank you.' Then she added, with a gallant effort at appearing unconcerned, 'I shall pick Ronald up at the Palmflower Club. He is sure to wait for me there.'

This was to the ladies. She did not even look at George. But that gentleman was still pressing in his attentions.

'At least let Clara go with you,' he said. 'You can send her on to Porchester Terrace afterwards.'

Edith simply took no notice, but walked off to the

victoria, which was drawn up behind the Stent equipage. Before he could argue with her, the carriage had driven off.

'Silly girl!' exclaimed George, when they had started. 'As if he would be at the Club. He is gone off with that woman, and I dare say he won't come back at all.'

The Cassonis did not answer, and Clara said, 'Hush, George!' It was a dreary drive home for all except George. He possessed *mentem consciam recti*, and hugged himself in the conviction that he had always thought Ronald a thorough bad lot. There must be a row after this. Edith would go to her uncle, and write to her father, and they would turn him out of the Bank. Poor thing! he felt a little sorry for her, for she had been gentle and polite; but he thought it just as well that her eyes should have been opened to her husband's true character.

Edith drove home in a sort of stupefied state. She

could not realize that her Ronald, her very own, had left her among these people, and coolly gone off with Lady Redbourne. It was too horrible. She still held in her hand the card he had sent her, and read it over and over again by the passing gleams of the street-lamps. There was just one glimmer of consolation in it. They 'insisted' on his dining with them, he said. No doubt they would not let him go. They were so pleased to have found him, found one so delightful to all, that they kept him for the evening. Perhaps, after all, the explanation was simple enough, and Ronald was not to blame. He had only thought that he would please his old friends by spending a few hours with them. There was no harm in it. But then that woman, that well-dressed coquette, who leant so confidingly on his arm when she saw them on the lawn before dinner! Eyes! She had wonderful eyes indeed, and she knew how to use them. So much even the unsophisticated innocent Edith had seen. And the kiss! surely it was a wicked story of George's! How she hated George Stent! with a hate far passing the hate of man.

At last the carriage drew up at her own door. She could scarcely wait till it was opened. Surely Ronald had returned! It was past eleven, and he had left Richmond long before they started. She remembered herself just in time, and did not ask the servant. A glance told her that he had not come back. The evening letters and the evening paper were still on the slab in the hall; his light overcoat was not hanging on its usual peg. She said as calmly as she could: 'Your master is at the Club. Do not wait up for him; he has the latch-key,' and went upstairs to her room.

She dismissed her maid, and undressed slowly, very slowly, pausing and sitting down for a while, listening intently for the front-door to open. The church-clock struck twelve when she laid her aching head on her pillow. Her tears had now dried up. Her pride began to assert itself. It was of no use to weep over a faithless husband. She must not show him how much she cared. She must put a good face on it, and dry her eyes, and be able to snap her fingers at him to-morrow, and upbraid him with a few scorching words. Scold? Of course she would not scold. Just a sharp biting sentence, which should bring him to his knees, and make him beg her pardon. She tried to make up such a sentence, but before she could arrive at a satisfactory one, her short period of pride came to an end, and she was once more the tearful despairing wife, impatiently listening for her husband's return, starting up at the slightest sound, and laying her head down again on the wet pillow in bitter disappointment.

One o'clock! Still no Ronald. A horrible thought struck her. Perhaps he would never return; perhaps he had left her for ever, because he could not love

her. No, surely, that was impossible. She remembered their happy weeks in Sicily. Surely Ronald, who had lain at her feet, and lovingly kissed her hand, and made much of her, and petted her, and had talked of his love in many soft southern twilights, could not thus have forsaken the woman for whom he had not scrupled to shed his blood. It was a wild fancy, an impossible dream. Yet she could not shake it off. As the minutes went slowly by it took a firmer hold of her, till in her agony she shrieked out :
' Oh, Ronald, come back to me, come back '

And there came an answer—as if her voice had penetrated through the walls—for she heard something, surely. It was the key turning in the lock. She was too impatient, too anxious to rest in bed, waiting. She rose and gently opened her door. This time there could be no mistake. She heard the chain put up and then Ronald's step sounded on the marble floor of the hall. There was a pause. He was removing his boots for fear of making a noise. Poor Edith! All her pride was gone ; all she felt was relief and joy at his return. Dear Ronald! he was afraid of disturbing her. It never struck her that he was sneaking into his own house like a thief in the night. She listened intently, with beating heart, as she heard him slowly ascend the stairs, which creaked as they always do creak when people want to be particularly quiet. She could not wait any longer when she heard him opening the door of his dressing-room. She forgot her dignity, her outraged pride, and her satirical sentence—even Lady Redbourne. She rushed out and fell into his arms, crying :

'Oh, Ronald dear! I am so glad you have come back! Kiss me, Ronald ; I thought you would never return to your poor Edith.'

CHAPTER XXVII.

FORGIVENESS.

HAD Edith been the most experienced and astute reader of men's hearts, she could not have humiliated Ronald more thoroughly than she did by following her simple loving impulse. She did not ask for a word of excuse from him. She kept his head pressed to her bosom, and kissed his short curls, and wept over him as if he were a prodigal son.

Her anticipations of the possible future had been so dark, her terror so dreadful, that she rejoiced to have him back on any terms. The tears of joy wiped out the record of his offence.

'Hush, hush!' she cried, when the wretched man

endeavoured to stammer some words of regret, and she put her little hand on his mouth; 'don't speak, darling! You are with me again, and that is enough. Kiss me, Ronald!'

Between laughter and tears, between joy and grief, she sobbed herself to sleep in the small hours, still clutching tightly hold of Ronald's hand, as if fearful that he might fly from her again.

He did not close his eyes all the night. Only that afternoon, on his way down to Richmond, Edith had shyly whispered something which ought to have made him ten times more loving, more careful of her than before. And within a few short hours of this announcement he had behaved in a manner certain not only to hurt her feelings, but to injure her health. Brutally, in short. If now his wife had spoken bitterly, nay, even if she had only been proud and silent, he would have been far less repentant. Even mute reproaches would have roused some sort of spirit of opposition—feeble and unfounded perhaps, but yet some resistance. As it was, he could do nothing but think over the wrong he had committed with bitterness in his heart.

He did not attempt to palliate his act by saying to himself that love is the master, and that he was in love with Lady Redbourne. He knew very well that if, even while with her, he had been suddenly told that they were both free, and that he could marry her next day, he would have hesitated. She was infinitely lovely, but she was morally far inferior to Edith. Now his brutal act stood out in its real character, by the lurid light of his conscience. He had been weakly carried away by a pair of black eyes, stylish dress, and the sentimental remembrance of his old love. Such seductions had sufficed to make him forget his sacred duty, and not only his duty, but even the laws of ordinary courtesy. He had been worse than fickle and weak ; he had been brutally rude to the woman whom, above all others, he was bound to respect, and, under the special circumstances, to cherish with especial care. He could not find the slightest excuse for his conduct, and was ashamed with a deeper shame than he had ever felt. He could scarcely control himself to lie quiet, for his anger impelled him to walk about and talk loudly, and call himself a contemptible wretch.

But though his shame and repentance were deep, though he made resolves which, he believed, would never be broken again, though he felt the burning coals which his wife had heaped on his head enter his brain, though his heart was full of remorse for his own wickedness, and full of tenderness for her, yet there was one feeling which never came over him, even once in those weary hours. Not once did he yearn to take Edith into his arms, and kiss her lips— not once did the love for her which he had acted so well for four weeks assume a real mastery over his heart. He turned towards her full of repentance, of sorrow for his own sin, and of tender, unspoken gratitude for the loving oblivion in which she wished to shroud it—but even though his whole soul was thus moved, there was no response to her warm love. His mind was full of affection for her ; in his heart there was tenderness and kindness—no more. And even now, when he recognised himself abased, and knew how infinitely noble was Edith's character in comparison to his own, he could understand, he could be grateful, he could admire, but, alas ! he felt that he could not love.

Ronald was in the dining-room that morning before Edith. When she came down she kissed both his eyes, and said simply :

'Never speak of it again, dear ! It was a bad dream —only a dream.'

She was pale, and looked tired; but her smile was bright, and there was no suggestion in her face, nor in her ways, that she wanted to pose as an ill-used wife. She had a loftier idea of forgiveness than most women. She not only forgave his offence, but wiped it out so entirely that things should be as if it had never been committed. It should not even shake her confidence in her husband.

Whilst she was dressing that morning she had had time to think, and had found a hundred excuses for Ronald—excuses which far surpassed in ingenuity any he could have invented for himself. First, of course, came the conduct of the lady. Nothing could be more abominable. She was an abandoned woman, who all but threw herself at his head. On Lady Redbourne Edith vented all the indignation of which she was capable; for Ronald she had nothing but sorrowful pity. Any man might have been carried away for a few moments by so clever, handsome, and unscrupulous a coquette. He was scarcely to blame, poor fellow! No doubt she, and the fast people with her, teased him about being tied to his dowdy wife, and would not let him go. She had married a handsome and attractive man, and how could she expect that he should appear handsome and attractive to her only? Other women liked him, and this was a very wicked woman, who evidently liked him very much, and respected neither her own marriage vows nor his. She knew that he was bitterly sorry now, poor fellow, and she thought he would love her more than ever. She would not risk the loss of his love by worrying him. Besides, why should she? It was not his fault. Probably if they had been with anyone else than the Stents, he would have come back to dinner. But she knew that George Stent always bored him, and drove him into ill-temper. She shuddered as she thought of George. So she went down to kiss her husband, and she gave her heart with her kiss.

While they were still at breakfast there was a ring at the front-door, and when the servant answered the bell, they heard a well-known voice in the passage.

Ronald changed colour, and put down the *Times.* Edith quickly jumped up from behind the urn, and came round the table.

'Ronald,' she whispered hurriedly, while deep blushes mantled her face and neck, 'that man is a wretch. He told me he had seen that woman kiss you last night. I know it wasn't true. But anyhow he was very wicked to tell me.'

Before Ronald could recover from his astonishment, the door opened, and George walked in. Edith had resumed her place. The visitor looked rather surprised to see the two seated comfortably at breakfast, as if nothing had occurred. He just nodded to Ronald, but said affectionately to Edith :

'How are you this morning, dear Edith ?' and held out his hand. She pretended not to see it.

'Quite well thank you,' she answered coldly.

' I thought I would come round and inquire at once, on my way to the City,' proceeded George.

Edith did not answer. He thought he must go on.

' It was very trying for you,' he said, with a severe look at Ronald; 'and we all felt so sorry.'

Edith's eyes flashed angrily, and the colour rose to her face. But she only said, ' There was no occasion to trouble. Ronald was waiting for me.' She felt very wicked as she uttered this terrible untruth. But what true woman will hesitate to tell a lie to shield the man she loves ?

' Oh !' said Mr. Stent rather incredulously, and glanced at Ronald, who looked annoyed.

The visitor had been standing all this time, and began to wonder that he was not asked to sit down. So he took a chair himself. Ronald resumed his *Times,* and Edith did not offer him a cup of tea. Still he would not take the hint.

' Ronald dear,' said his wife, after a short silence,

31—2

'shall you have time for the Academy this afternoon ?'

This was said more sweetly and affectionately than
usual. There was a loving inflection in her voice
which, under ordinary circumstances, would have
been reserved for a *tête-à-tête.* And in order that
there might be no mistake, she came round to Ronald,
and drew up a chair close to him on the side away
from George, who was sitting near the door. Ronald
understood at once. He laid down the paper and
answered, looking at her, and therefore almost turning
his back to George.

'I think I can manage it, darling. I might get
away by four o'clock.'

With an audacity for which he would not have
given her credit, Edith then put her arm round her
husband's neck, and whispered into his ear ; and what
she said was, 'I wish that snake would go !' But it
looked as if she had kissed him.

George Stent began to feel uncomfortable.

'Are you going to the City ?' he asked Ronald.

'Yes, by-and-by.'

'I will wait, and walk with you. I wish to speak to you,' said George solemnly. Could he believe his eyes ? He actually saw Ronald's arm steal round Edith's waist. After such a scandalous affair as that of last night, and before a third person too ! It was incredible.

Seeing that they could not get rid of their unwelcome guest, Ronald hastened to finish breakfast and to start. Edith brought a rosebud, which she fastened in his button-hole affectionately. She whispered at the same time :

'Don't give in to him, Ronald But don't quarrel with him ; he is dangerous.'

'You need have no fear, Edith dear,' replied he, stooping to give her one last kiss.

When they had closed the door behind them, Ronald at once began:

'What have you to say, George?'

'I consider myself entitled to ask for an explanation,' was the reply.

'Of what?'

'Of your conduct last night.'

'Of my conduct last night?' What is there to explain, please?' inquired Ronald, staring hard at his brother-in-law.

'Why, everything!' replied George.

'Don't talk nonsense. Say what you want to say, and have done with it. I have nothing to explain.'

'Nothing!' exclaimed Mr. Stent indignantly. 'Do you call it nothing to leave *my* dinner-party, to which I had invited you, and go off with that fast Lady Redbourne?—to insult me and Clara, and your wife——'

'Stop, please,' interrupted Ronald. 'You may ask me for an explanation or, at least, an apology for my having left your little party so abruptly. But do not bring my wife in. She has nothing to do with it, and

I have no explanation to give you about my conduct towards her, nor indeed in any respect whatever.'

'Indeed ?' said George sarcastically ; ' no explanation ?'

' None. I beg to apologize for not having dined with you ; I was unable to do so, as my friends, whom I had not seen for years, would not let me go. Do you accept the apology ?'

' So far of course I must,' replied George very doubtfully, ' about the dinner I mean.'

' Very well, then, old man,' again interrupted Ronald, ' let us shake hands, and say no more about it. Now I must take a hansom, as I am late. Will you come too ?'

' Wait a minute,' said George, who had taken Ronald's hand in a feeble, confused sort of way; ' this is not all.'

' It's all you will get out of me,' answered Ronald,

laughing. 'There, old chap, do not flurry yourself. You have got your apology, and there's an end of it.'

His brother-in-law did not like this flippant joviality at all. 'Ronald,' he went on gravely, 'having married your sister, I am entitled to make some strictures as to your conduct.'

'You are not entitled to anything, George, except to drive into the City with me, if you like.'

'As a member of the family, Ronald, I cannot stand by silently and see you kiss another woman, and drive off with her!'

'Are you off your head?' asked Ronald quite seriously, 'or did you have too much wine last night?'

'Neither, as you well know.'

'I know nothing about it. But you are talking arrant nonsense, George.'

'It is not nonsense, and I require an explanation,' persisted he.

'An explanation of your visions! Pooh, George!

Hansom !" shouted Ronald. The cab pulled up to the curb.

'Look here, George,' said Ronald to his brother-in-law, who could not at once muster an answer to what appeared a flat and audacious denial of what he had seen. 'The fact is, you must have taken my share of the champagne as well as your own. You were evidently as drunk as an owl. Lombard Street, cabby, and look sharp. Ta-ta!'

George stared after the cab in mute amazement. He, George Stent, had been accused of being drunk! and by a young man of the most dissolute character, too! What audacity! Yet, by the behaviour of the couple this morning, one could certainly suppose that they were on the best terms, nay, very much in love with each other; and yet surely Edith was not such an absolute fool as to have already forgiven what took place last night! Impossible. But did it take place? Was there a kiss at all? He had never been drunk in his life, and it was an insult to say he had; but had he been mistaken in the couple? He raised his hat and passed his hand over his forehead, thoughtfully, then slowly turned Citywards.

CHAPTER XXVIII.

THE VEHM.

OF course George Stent turned for guidance and counsel to the clan. Ronald's charge rankled in his breast, and was too bitter to bear in silence. He had always consulted the family when in a difficulty, and he would do so now. But before laying the matter before the Grand Council, he would have a quiet talk with his father. Could he leave matters as they were? Ronald was absolutely not to be trusted, and very much worse than they had supposed. For he was not only devoid of all moral sense himself, but actually insulted his own relatives who were virtuous.

When Mr. Stent senior heard the tale he felt

extremely indignant. The tenderest toes of the Stent family were trodden on. All the Stents loved their wives and each other's wives, and the sacredness of family ties was to them a very watchword. But as old Mr. Stent had not been told to his face that he had been drunk, he was of course less offended than his son, who described with great bitterness both the evening at Richmond and the interview of that morning. Mr. Stent advised that George should make one more effort to induce Ronald to repent. It was not, he thought, in accordance with Christian charity to condemn and punish him without giving him another chance. Condemned and punished he should be, if he refused to avail himself of it.

So father and son determined to go round to Lombard Street at an early date, and have a quiet chat with the criminal.

Things in Lombard Street were not going smoothly on that morning. Certain ugly rumours had lately reached the ears of the partners, and to-day there were letters which seemed to confirm them.

'I do not like the way the Wendovers are going on, sir,' said Ronald to Mr. Woodall.

'Nor do I. But I believe they are good enough.'

'They will go if there's any general fall in prices.'

'What makes you think so?' asked Mr. Woodall.

'I believe they have taken up none but really first-rate schemes, and you know how strong they are.'

Then Ronald showed his senior the result of his journeys, and his private inquiries; and Mr. Woodall was surprised to find that Wendovers had bolstered up several concerns which might turn out prosperous if the present inflation lasted a couple of months longer, but which would certainly come down if there were any reaction. They decided to decline Wendovers' paper, though it was a ticklish thing to risk offending so influential and powerful a firm. After much consideration they decided to restrict all their operations, a decision which Mr. Edward Woodall took with much regret, and only on Ronald's earnest solicitation. Never, said the senior, had there been such chances of making large sums of money. But Ronald stuck to his opinion that things could not go on long in the same smooth and prosperous manner, and that their duty was to increase their cash reserve at the Bank of England, to discount very little paper, and that only if absolutely above suspicion, and to keep clear of new companies. Soon after this decision had been arrived at, the chief clerk came in with a bundle of shares.

'Mr. George Stent has sent round for five thousand on a hundred Chios wines,' he said.

'Chios wines!' exclaimed Ronald. 'Let's see them.'

'What are they quoted at?' asked Mr. Woodall.

'Ten to twelve premium, sir.'

'They are fifty-pound shares, are they not?' asked Mr. Woodall.

'Yes, sir?'

'How is the market? and for how long does he want the money?'

'Till next settling day. The market is lively and rising, sir,' replied the clerk.

'Leave the shares here for five minutes,' said Ronald; 'we will let you know directly.' When the clerk had closed the door, he turned to Mr. Woodall:

'This is one of Wendovers' companies, uncle. Charles Wendover and young Glaston are both on the Board. I do not believe the shares are worth a sovereign each.'

'But he only wants fifty pounds, and they are quoted at 61½,' said Mr. Woodall.

'Yes; but they may go down to forty to-morrow, and to thirty next day, if anything should go wrong. I should refuse point-blank. Look at the prospectus!'

'Do as you please,' said his uncle, after glancing through the papers which Ronald placed before him.

'I believe you are right.' Ronald took up the bundle of shares and summoned George Stent's clerk into the waiting-room.

'Tell Mr. Stent,' said he, 'that we are very sorry we cannot oblige him. We cannot advance anything on these securities. They are not the class of paper we like.'

When George Stent received this message, his anger knew no bounds. What ! refuse an advance on valuable security to him, whose word in the City was as good as a bank-note ? Not only was the company supported by such unexceptionable people as Wendovers; but even had it been a doubtful success, he, George Stent, was good for ten times the amount asked for. He asked his clerk to whom he had spoken, and the latter replied that he had only seen Mr. Lascelles. It was, therefore, an intentional insult, which, added to the former ones, made the cup of Ronald's misdeeds overflow. The clan was summoned for the next evening. The questions submitted were the following:

First: A member of the family had been accused by Mr. Ronald Lascelles of having been tipsy; was this accusation true or false?

Secondly: Mr. Lascelles had misbehaved himself in the grossest manner at Richmond, by abruptly leaving Mr. George Stent's dinner-party, and spending the whole evening with a set of fast friends, ending by driving off with a coquette called Lady Redbourne.

Thirdly: If the accusation of drunkenness was an unfounded one, Mr. Lascelles had also kissed the said Lady Redbourne.

Fourthly: Mr. Ronald Lascelles had refused the usual banking accommodation to Mr. George Stent, and had thereby cast doubts on his credit and seriously inconvenienced him.

Fifthly: What should the family do under the circumstances?

Poor Clara was summoned to give evidence on the first question. She did not know why she was called into the dining-room to meet all the male members of her husband's family, or possibly she might have stood up for her brother even before this august assemblage. But Mr. Stent senior simply asked her whether George was tipsy at Richmond on Tuesday night.

'Of course not,' answered she, blushing and looking very unhappy. 'What an idea!'

'Ronald says I was,' observed George insidiously.

'No, certainly you were not,' repeated Clara, feeling suddenly quite angry with her brother, which was exactly what George had calculated on.

'Your brother did not dine with you?' asked Mr. Stent senior.

'No. We were very sorry. He went away with some friends,' replied Clara, unwilling to enter into further details.

'That will do, dear,' said the old man. 'You may

go to the drawing-room. We will join you by-and-by.'

The counsel then deliberated. As it was established that George had been sober, obviously charges two and three were proved, and their gravity was undoubted. There could be no possible excuse. The Stents had taken a snake to their bosom. Ronald was not only an immoral character, but he was actuated by hostility and malice to the clan, as was proved by his two social offences and the grave commercial insult which he had last committed. Not a voice was raised in his defence, though Mr. William Stent, who respected the aristocracy even more than his brothers and cousins, suggested that as the person he had flirted with was a lady of title, there might be some excuse for his being carried away. But all agreed that, even if that were so, it was no palliation of the false charge of drunkenness Ronald had brought against George, still less a reason for refusing to ad-

vance five thousand pounds on Chios wines. A
verdict of guilty having been recorded on all counts,
the clan then discussed at length what sentence
should be passed on the all-unconscious Ronald.
Like the tribunal of the *Vehm*, the secret order went
forth at midnight, and every member of the clan
became an officer charged to execute it.

Ronald began to suppose that the whole thing had
blown over, and that he should hear no more about it.
He had yet to learn that a false step always has evil
results sooner or later. It is never entirely without
its consequences, though we sometimes, in our pur-
blindness, fail to recognise them as such.

Edith called on Clara in the middle of the day,
when she knew that her objectionable husband was
sure to be in the City. Mrs. George received her
sadly and tearfully. There was something in the wind,
and she knew there was, though not the nature of the
intended blow ; but the poor creature had become too

much of a Stent to make any endeavour to divert it. She could only ask Edith dolefully how she was, and on receiving a reassuring reply, inquire further, in a whisper, how she was getting on at home.

'Why capitally, dear,' replied Edith, taking the bull by the horns. 'Why should we not? Do you think I am angry with Ronald for having dined with his friends the other night? Not a bit. I was silly to be upset at the time—I have forgotten all about it now.'

Thus she loyally stood to her guns, and Clara was puzzled, like her husband when he called on the delinquent. But she could not forget that Ronald had accused George of being tipsy—an imprudent charge which had sent his own sister into the enemy's camp. She was, however, too timid to mention this offence, and finding that Edith did not require consolation and sympathy, talked of her health, and of the event which was approaching. An undoubted constraint arose between them, and both were glad when the visit came to an end.

Clara was more than once tempted to warn her brother through his wife, but she lacked courage and the knowledge to do so. She would only have warned him against an unknown danger, and she would have done so at the expense of her loyalty to her husband. So she held her peace.

Edith said nothing of her visit. Her anger against George Stent was as deep as ever, and she quite determined that the relations between the two families should in future be of the most limited nature. She need not have feared a renewal of their old intimacy. For the male Stents had decided that Ronald was a black sheep whom no washing could whiten, and that he must be excluded from the virtuous Stent fold.

On the Monday following Mr. Stent senior and George called at the Bank, and asked to see Ronald in private.

He held out his hand to the old gentleman, who pretended not to see it. 'This was sufficient to put him on his guard. So placing chairs for the visitors, he leaned against the chimney-piece and waited for them to speak.

'Mr. Lascelles,' began the elder man, 'this is a painful visit.'

'Indeed ?' asked Ronald.

'Yes, sir,' continued he. 'Of course you know why we have come ?'

'I have no idea.'

Mr. Stent looked at his son, amazed at the sinner's audacity.

'Surely, Mr. Lascelles, it is plain enough,' he went on rather warmly.

'Please tell me,' said Ronald.

'Sir, you have grossly insulted my son and the party he invited to Richmond——'

'I apologized for that,' interrupted Ronald.

'In apologizing you aggravated your offence by bringing an unjustifiable charge against George !'

'Charge ?'

'Yes. You dared to say that he was intoxicated.'

'George talked some nonsense about a married lady whom I deeply respect,' replied Ronald, smiling; 'and I concluded he had had a little too much wine. But I did not mean to say that he was drunk and disorderly ! It was not a case of forty shillings or a month. He was only a little excited, you know.'

It was Ronald's old flippant way, which was likely to be more harmful to him now than it had ever been before. Nor could he help the allusion to Lady Redbourne. He would not have her abused by the Stents, had she been even very much worse than she was. The speech was intensely irritating to father and son, and Ronald's manner still more.

'Sir! we have not come to be laughed at, nor to hear you talking of that *person*——'

'Mr. Stent,' interrupted Ronald, 'be good enough not to allude to the lady.'

'Your conduct compels me to do so,' said Mr. Stent. 'But it is unnecessary to dwell further on your behaviour to your poor wife.'

'That is nobody's business but our own!' exclaimed Ronald hotly, 'and if you persist in interfering in matters in which you have no concern I shall be obliged to ask you to leave the Bank.'

This was the grossest insult of all. Thus to threaten two Stents, who were received with attention and obsequious civility in every office in the City, and whose very presence was an honour!

'We had better go, father,' said George. 'I told you it was of no use. He is quite hardened.'

'Give the young man one more chance,' said Mr. Stent. 'Mr. Lascelles, do I understand that you refuse to apologize for the three separate insults you have offered our family, not to speak of your extremely

offensive language to-day? Beware of the consequences of your stiffneckedness.'

'Mr. Stent,' answered Ronald, 'I am really only
aware of one offence, which I have apologized for—that
of leaving your son's party. It is not worth all the
fuss you make about it. But as you are an older man
than I am, I will, if it pleases you, repeat that apology.
I am very sorry for my rudeness on that occasion.'

'Come, I thought you would be reasonable,' said
Mr. Stent, quite pleased, while George began to fear
that his enemy would escape him. He determined
not to let him off so easily, and therefore touched
him on the tenderest spot.

'You know I was not drunk, Ronald,' he exclaimed
roughly; 'you must withdraw that insult. You know
I saw you kiss that woman.'

'Nothing of the sort,' cried Ronald. 'As you
repeat that libel, which, by-the-by, I advise you to
keep to yourself, otherwise you will get your head

punched, I must also repeat that you must have been drunk or mad.'

'You have spoilt everything, George!' exclaimed Mr. Stent regretfully.

'But I *did* see them, father,' persisted George.

'Now, sir,' said Ronald, advancing towards his brother-in-law, who shrank towards the door, 'I will not chastise you at once, because, unfortunately, you married my sister ; but I warn you at your peril to repeat your charge. If I hear that you have done so, I will horsewhip you publicly, though you may be my brother-in-law. Do you understand ?'

George was as pale as death, and trembled all over. His father stepped between them. 'That will do, Mr. Lascelles,' he said. 'You are, I am sorry to see, incorrigible. You must not be surprised at our withdrawing our confidence.'

'Withdraw whatever you d—n please,' answered Ronald hotly. 'Good-morning.'

CHAPTER XXIX.

A RUN.

RONALD paced up and down the room impatiently when he had closed the door behind them. His temper was much ruffled, but, angry as he was, his common-sense stepped in and warned him too late that he ought to have been more cautious. In less than five minutes he regretted that he had given way to his indignation. His knowledge of George Stent's character ought to have kept him cool. He flattered himself that he could see through that very proper, regular, and pedantic young man, and that he had long ago detected the innate meanness of the character which was so well disguised in apparent smugness and good-nature. Yet he had neglected his knowledge, and had courted the danger which that knowledge ought to have taught him to avoid. He believed that George Stent would not hesitate to injure him by every possible means, and that his spite would vent itself in secret attacks on the Bank which no skill and no audacity would enable Ronald to parry. He perceived, now it was too late, that he had no right to assume so defiant a tone. His conduct would affect not himself only, but others, and a consideration of the possible consequences to the Woodalls ought to have made him more conciliatory. He had given a flat denial to George Stent's accusation, though he knew it was true. He had retorted by the counter-charge of drunkenness, which he knew to be false. Perhaps, according to the unwritten code of honour which has to some extent taken the place of the ten commandments among men of the world, Ronald might be justified in shielding Lady Redbourne by a falsehood.　But no code justified his making an irritating and groundless charge against a man who might seriously injure the Bank of which he was a junior partner.　He now felt that he had been not only rash and imprudent, but also morally wrong.　A sudden impulse came over him to rush after the Stents and apologize.　If he had followed it at once perhaps many difficulties might have been avoided. But at that moment Mr. Woodall summoned him into his room, and a precious half-hour was lost in discussing other matters.　Before these were settled, the chief clerk came in with a long face.

'Will you look at these cheques, sir ?' said he to Mr. Woodall.　There were three of them, all presented at the same time and all to the same effect.　The three Stent firms withdrew their balances.

Mr. Woodall made no remark.　He was not in the habit of conversing freely with any one in the Bank except with Ronald.　The chief clerk was an admirable machine, but both the senior partners knew that he was only a machine. Had he been capable of anything better than running smoothly and noiselessly, driving the other wheels with him daily from nine o'clock to five, it is probable that Ronald would not have gained his present post so easily.

'Well, pay them,' said Mr. Woodall.

'It's on account of our refusing the Chios wine shares, I'm afraid, sir,' the clerk ventured to remark.

'Never mind what it's for, Mr. Radlet. We can't help it now.'

Mr. Radlet lingered a moment, as if anxious that his principals should make some suggestion to turn away the wrath of the Stents and keep their balances. But they made none. So he departed unwillingly to honour the cheques. The door had scarcely closed when Ronlad spoke.

'This is not only because of the Chios shares, sir. I am now very sorry indeed, but I fear I have mortally offended George Stent and the old gentleman. May I make a clean breast of it ?'

Then he proceeded to relate the whole story as briefly as he could. Blushing, he told of his folly at Richmond; with a flush of anger he recounted George Stent's morning visit. It was not pleasant to have to tell Edith's uncle how ill he had behaved to Edith; and more than once he stammered and hesitated in his tale.

At first Mr. Woodall stared and interrupted him, not understanding how so domestic a matter should affect the Bank. But Ronald went on bravely, and in his anxiety to take all the blame on himself, and to place Edith's gentle forbearance in its true colours, he made his own case even worse than it was. Mr. Woodall shook his head more than once, and was disinclined to believe that so old and experienced a man as Mr. Stent senior would convert a tiff between Ronald and his son into a formidable family and business quarrel. But when he heard of the interview which had just concluded, his incredulity ceased, though his wonder increased.

'Now, sir—now that you know all—shall I go round to Stent Brothers, and the rest of them, and apologize? I will do exactly as you think best.'

'It would be a most disagreeable thing to do, Ronald,' said Mr. Woodall.

'Never mind that,' replied the young man; 'I must put my pride in my pocket. I have made an awful ass of myself, and I'm ready to do my best to put matters straight, if I can. The Bank must not lose through my folly.'

'I would not ask you to do it, my boy,' said the senior kindly.

'I know you would not, sir. But if it is a wise step to take, I will take it. Please not to consider my feelings at all.'

'It is difficult to know what to do,' replied Mr.

Woodall, thoughtfully. ' If they had not been in such
a hurry to close their account I should say, " Go by all
means.   You've made a blunder, so beg their pardon
for it."   But you see the matter is almost public property now.   If you apologize, they will think it is
because the Bank wants their money, and it would
never do to allow them to fancy that.'

' No, indeed,' acquiesced Ronald.

Mr. Woodall leant back in his chair and chewed the
end of the little stumpy pencil he always carried in
his waistcoat pocket.

' You see,' he said, after a few minutes' reflection,
'if you go to them now, they'll think *I*'m apologizing ;
that Woodalls, in fact, are apologizing.   Now, we've
nothing to apologize for.   I would not lend money on
those shares to-day, any more than I would last week.'

' Far less,' remarked Ronald.   ' What we have
heard since about Wendovers' is not reassuring.'

' Certainly not,' agreed Mr. Woodall.   ' In fact, I

believe your caution did us a good turn.' After a pause he added : 'No. You must *not* go to them, Ronald. We must do our best to get on without them. We managed to exist without the Stents before you joined us, and I dare say we shall manage again.'

'All I fear, sir,' said Ronald, 'is that they may do the Bank harm.'

'How?' inquired Mr. Woodall. 'Not by withdrawing their balances? Why, the total is scarcely worth thinking about.'

'No,' answered Ronald ; 'not by that alone. I think they will walk about everywhere and injure us in every possible way.'

'I don't believe it,' replied Mr. Woodall. 'You are a little prejudiced, Ronald, and I'm not surprised ; but you are wrong about this. George Stent may be a fussy, meddlesome ass, but he is not such a scoundrel as to try and ruin the Bank.'

'Indeed, I hope not, for it would be all my fault !

But I fear he is worse than you think, and I should like to take every step your experience can suggest. There is a big storm coming, anyhow, Stents or no Stents; and though we've already shortened sail, I would be more careful than ever.'

'By all means!' said Mr. Woodall. 'We'll look out for squalls.'

The big storm, however, if storm there was, did not approach very rapidly. On the contrary, during the next few days every speculative security was in demand, and several new ventures were brought out. But though the financial sky appeared clear enough, the private affairs of Woodalls were not prospering. When, one afternoon, Mr. Edward Woodall made some business calls, he read strange news on the faces of some who called themselves his friends. Not a word was said to him that did not imply absolute confidence; not a hint was dropped in his presence suggestive of any doubts in the stability of the Bank.

But Mr. Woodall had not been in the City for over thirty years for nothing. He discovered more from what men did not say than from what they said; he read more on men's faces than he learnt from their words. And when he returned to the Bank a quarter of an hour before closing time, he found the place much fuller than usual. There was quite a crowd of persons before the counter of the paying cashiers. And in that crowd there was far more impatience to hand in strips of blue paper than was usually displayed.

'What is the matter, Ronald?' he asked anxiously, as he stepped into the private room, where he found the young man poring over the big books.

'Well, sir,' replied he, 'Cosgroves, Hopkinsons, Davis, and several more have closed their accounts. The private customers are drawing out pretty fast.'

'Anything to hurt?' asked Mr. Woodall.

'Nothing to hurt *yet*, sir,' answered Ronald. 'It's five minutes to four, and there won't be much mischief done now.   But I went round to the Continental just now with Walker's bills, so as to have something in hand, and they said they would rather not discount any more at present.'

'Good heavens!' exclaimed Mr. Woodall. 'Why, Walker is as good as the Bank of England, and do you mean to say they would not take his paper with our name behind it ?'

'That is the state of the case, sir.   Their manager kept me waiting twenty minutes, and then said that he was sorry he could not oblige me; but they were restricting their operations.'

'Bosh !' cried Mr. Woodall. 'Restricting their operations, indeed !   I know better than that.   But I do not understand it in the least.'

'I am sorry to say that I do,' said Ronald. 'The Stents have done it.'

'Done what ?   What does it all mean ?'

'It means, sir, A RUN ON THE BANK.'

CHAPTER XXX.

THE WEST-END.

In the City it was close and almost suffocating on that June evening. The atmosphere was yellow, the sky dull and coppery. The narrow streets were hot as the flues of a furnace, the paving-stones and asphalte burnt the soles of the busy foot-passengers. When the shutters were put up at Woodalls' Bank, and when the great front-door was closed, Ronald felt as if he would choke. Light seemed to be shut out, not for that evening only, but for ever. Mr. Woodall might think that all this was only a momentary alarm, a fright among the customers which would quickly subside ; but Ronald thought he knew better.

During the last twenty-four hours, sinister rumours about the Bank had rapidly spread throughout the City. People who had known both the Woodalls for years denied that there was any foundation for them, but they were so persistently reasserted on what appeared good authority, that the faith of the Bank's best friends began to be shaken. It seemed to Ronald that a fearful and disproportionate punishment was being meted out to him for his Richmond folly. He would willingly have suffered the penalty himself, but that others, innocent of any transgression, should be dragged down into wretchedness with him seemed too unjust to be borne. His work, his energy, his untiring exertions for the Bank had all been worse than wasted. How often he had declared to himself that Woodalls should never repent their bargain, and should never regret having made an impecunious young man their partner!

Many times even in the last few weeks he had

looked down the columns of figures with satisfaction, and had whispered to himself that youthful energy, combined with caution, would prove more valuable to the firm than capital! How he had slaved during the past months to collect information, and to find out whom the Bank should trust and to whom they should refuse credit! What a mass of work he had gone through! Was the fruit of all this labour to be dust and ashes? It appeared likely. For though the Woodalls could easily have met all the claims of their private customers, the sudden withdrawal of confidence by the large business firms could not but be fatal. There was no time to realize, and the very securities which would have been as good as Bank of England notes under ordinary circumstances became little better than waste paper, in consequence of the alarm among their clients. Though Mr. Edward Woodall did not share all Ronald's fears, he went out immediately after banking hours to call on some old friends, and try to obtain assistance and restore confidence. Ronald remained in the stuffy office, almost gasping for relief and fresh air.

But in the West there was no gloom on this hot summer's evening. The Park was at its brightest and gayest. The light westerly wind blew the smoke and fog over to the City, and the thinnest of mists scarcely veiled the blue sky. The Row was full of riders ; the Drive was fuller still of smart carriages. Gaily dressed people crowded the paths, and ladies in cool, fresh summer garments occupied all the chairs. Lady Redbourne pulled up her well-bred chestnut cobs, whose arched necks were flecked with foam, and stopped the phaeton close to the rails. She was handsome, well dressed, fashionable, rich, and a Countess ; therefore her carriage was soon surrounded by a knot of loungers. A few ladies stopped in their walk for an interchange of civilities, and then passed on. The men, however, remained longer, striving for a few words from so

charming and attractive a woman. For a beginner in
London society, it was a distinction to have the honour
of knowing Lady Redbourne, and to be seen talking
to her in the Park was equivalent to a certificate of
good birth and good breeding. Lady Redbourne looked
round for Ronald, who, on that eventful Richmond
evening, had promised to meet her in the Park whenever he could get away from the City. But one fine
evening had followed another, and Ronald had not
kept his promise. The beautiful American never
suspected the real reason of his absence. She would
not have believed for a moment that one of her old
admirers—perhaps the only one for whom she had
entertained more than a mere passing fancy—would
voluntarily deprive himself of the pleasure of seeing
her. A doubt of her own powers of attraction never
entered her head. Yet she was a clever woman of the
world, and knew more about business and money
matters than most people supposed. She was per-

fectly aware that Lascelles had no money of his own, and, as she said, 'putting two and two together,' she had formed a theory, thoroughly satisfactory to herself, which accounted for his having married Edith, and also accounted for his absence. He was, she thought, quite right to embrace the opportunity and the banker's daughter; and being an able and intelligent young man, he was also quite right to work hard in his new position. Poor fellow! he must be still simmering over his big books in the hot City, instead of leaning over the rails in the green, breezy Park to talk to her! So Ronald was forgiven, though she wondered that he had not written even a conventional note of regret. Perhaps he would turn up to-day, and explain himself. She glanced over the heads of the men who surrounded her, and tried to find the well-known pleasant face in the crowd behind. She did not see him whom she sought, but her beautiful dark eyes rested for a moment on the faultlessly attired figure of Mr. Munden, who instantly raised his white hat and pushed his way towards the phaeton.

Lady Redbourne bowed languidly, while the new-comer eagerly approached her.

'How are you to-day, Lady Redbourne?' he inquired. 'You look irresistible, as usual, and those cobs are improving every day——'

'Tell me something amusing, Mr. Munden,' said her ladyship. 'I am bored. I have not heard anything but stale jokes and tiresome compliments.'

'When people see you, they forget all the rest of the world,' answered Munden.

'Don't be foolish. Have you no news?'

'Oh yes!' answered he. 'Mrs. Roade has run away with young Hexham, and Roade is sending all the London detectives after them.'

'Oh! I have heard that three times already,' replied Lady Redbourne, half concealing a yawn. 'What a fool she is! Quiet, Soda! Can't you stand still?' she continued, addressing one of her cobs.

'Creole will win next Wednesday,' Munden went on, trying to think of something interesting for the exacting lady.

'He is not good enough for the Derby,' replied Lady Redbourne. 'I do not think he can stay the course.'

'There is nothing better, and Winchester is backing him for a fortune.'

'So much the worse for Lord Winchester! You will see that Uxbridge will beat him.'

'I will lay you the odds he does not, Lady Redbourne,' said Munden.

'What in?' asked her ladyship.

'Anything I can afford,' replied the gentleman. 'Tenners, if you like.'

'No?' answered Lady Redbourne; 'that would not be fair. I hate betting for money. I tell you what we will do. If you lose, you shall give us a picnic somewhere——'

'And if I win, Lady Redbourne ?' he interrupted.

'Then you must depend on my generosity !' she answered, laughing. 'You shall have a park hack, or a T-cart, or some other toy that will please you !'

'Done !' exclaimed Munden, rapidly calculating the position of the horses in the betting, which gave him about three to one the best of it, on the supposition that the picnic would cost as much as the hack, which would scarcely be the case.

'Where have you been to-day ?' asked Lady Red-bourne, as she saw that her cavalier was still anxious to continue the conversation.

'Oh, slaving in the City as usual,' he replied.

'Slaving ! It's much better than idling about doing nothing, like most of the men one sees about. You need not be ashamed of it. Anything new in the City ?'

'Nothing particular. Oh! I beg pardon, though. There's something wrong with one of the banks. I don't suppose you care about that.'

'Why not?' asked she. 'I look after my own money, you know. Lord Redbourne has nothing to do with it. So I am always anxious to hear what the banks are about.'

'By-the-bye,' continued Munden, maliciously, 'you should be interested in this one, too. I forgot that you were fond of young Lascelles.'

'Mr. Munden!' exclaimed Lady Redbourne, flushing.

'Oh! I don't mean anything. Only it's his bank; at least, the one he calls himself a partner in.'

'What?' asked she. 'Has it failed?' She waited almost breathlessly for an answer.

'No,' he replied, 'not yet; but they say it will go. There was a run on it this afternoon.'

'Have they been speculating, then?' inquired Lady Redbourne.

'Certainly not. It's the last thing old Woodall would do; and they say in the City that young Lascelles is as sharp as a needle, and as cautious as a Scotchman. Oh no! I believe there is some spite at the bottom of it; jealousy of some one, I suppose. But of course when once people begin to lose confidence, everybody draws their money out, and then the concern must go.'

'Without any fault of the partners?' asked her ladyship. 'That is horrible!'

'So it is,' assented Munden. 'But in the City, you know, like everywhere else, it's the devil take the hindmost.'

'Then Mr. Lascelles will be ruined?'

'I suppose so,' said Munden calmly, 'unless some one lends them a big lump. And that,' continued he, with a light smile, 'isn't very likely just now. Sorry for your friend, Lady Redbourne.'

'Oh, never mind my friend, Mr. Munden. We

will go on, Frank,' she said, speaking to her groom.
And with a slight nod to the golden youths around,
Lady Redbourne gave the cobs their head, turned out
through Albert Gate and drove thoughtfully up
Piccadilly. Where she drove at this advanced hour
of the afternoon may presently appear.

Poor Edith had an anxious time that evening
Following her uncle's instructions, Ronald whispered
no hint to her of impending misfortune. But his
harassed looks and the lines of anxiety on his forehead were easily detected by her when he returned
home just before seven, and announced that he must
at once start for the North on business. For it had
been decided that the best chance of weathering the
storm was to get the Manchester and Leeds people to
help them. For many years Woodalls in London had
advanced money on piece goods and iron-work which
went out to Italy; and Woodall of Portino or their
agents had been paid when the merchandise was sold.

Therefore to the manufacturers whom he had more than once helped over difficulties Mr. Edward Woodall naturally turned when he himself required help. It would not do for him to leave the Bank, and Ronald had made the acquaintance of all these friends during his recent journeys. So, although the senior partner thought that they might possibly pull through without assistance, yet he accepted Ronald's offer to go North with ready warmth. If anything were to be done, it must be done at once; so it was agreed that the young man should start for Leeds by the night mail, and if he were not entirely successful there, should proceed to Manchester the next afternoon, unless recalled by a telegram from London. Ronald had an hour in which to dine, pack, and make his adieux. His attempts at cheerfulness, at an assumption of indifference, as if this journey were no more than all the others had been, were an entire failure. With the keen eye of a faithful wife, Edith saw through it all; saw that he was frightfully anxious and nervous, saw that some danger impended. He parried her questions as well as he could, but only succeeded in showing that he did not wish to answer, not in dispelling her fears. If he had only been in entire sympathy with Edith, if he had loved her as she loved him, he would have told her everything without hesitation; for he would have known that the loss of money was a misfortune she could contemplate with calmness, and face with courage. It would be very disagreeable, no doubt, but Edith could never have brought herself to consider mere poverty to be a great calamity. In comparison with the catastrophe which she had feared on that Richmond evening, even the ruin of the Bank would have appeared insignificant. If she had Ronald, what would it matter whether they had four hundred a year to live on, or three thousand?

But Edith did not know what was the matter, and, far from suspecting the truth, her anxiety took quite a different turn. Was Ronald engaged in some adventure connected with the fascinating woman whom he had met a fortnight ago? Had that lady, whose attractions she felt to be far greater than her own, persuaded her husband into some hasty step which would bring misfortune and disgrace on himself, and death to her?

When Ronald's cab drove off, she felt as she felt on that dreadful night—an awful fear lest he should never return! It was of no use arguing with herself and telling herself that it could only be business, and nothing more; that he had often been to Leeds before, and had safely returned to her in a day or two; that Ronald himself had said he was going on business. Terrible fear still haunted her, and was proof against all reasoning.

Once she had almost decided to drive off to Wimbledon and see her Uncle Edward. But then it struck her that she would make a fool of herself, and of Ronald as well, by surprising the family at ten o'clock at night with an inquiry as to her husband's whereabouts. She was to have gone to a party on that evening, but she had not the courage to face a crowd of fashionable people. She remained at home, and retired to what should have been rest, anxious, sleepless, listening for every sound, and her heart beating whenever a carriage drove down the short street.

END OF VOL. II.

BILLING AND SONS, PRINTERS, GUILDFORD.